THE CASE
OF THE
GOOD DEED

Jim Shon & Masa Hagino

Paperback: 978-1-7338331-0-3
eBook: 978-1-7338331-1-0

HAWAII
INSIGHT
BOOKS

162 Forest Ridge Way
HONOLULU, HI 96822
United States

Contents

Main Characters

Dr. Dayton Apo, Director, The Cook Museum

Charlie C. Chang – a Honolulu Police Detective

Kirk Daniels – a young researcher at the Cook Museum

Joe and Molly (Mai Tai) Davis – owners and managers of a small walk up apartment

Henry Doyle – a City bus driver

Yoshiro "Moto" Fujimoto – a restaurant owner

Sheri Ishihara – a young resident of Kaka'ako, girlfriend of Kekoa Potter

Julie – a bar owner in Chinatown

Peter Kalani – a projectionist at a local theater, Uncle of Kekoa Potter

Kawika…a Hawai'ian resident of Honolulu in the 19th century

Kono – Shilling's assistant

Zoe Lee – a young reporter

Dr. Jon Miller – a University of Hawai'i Professor

Kekoa Potter – a young resident of Kaka'ako, nephew of Peter Kalani

Leighton Thomas, Chief of Staff for the Kaka'ako Commission

Sally, the Cat Lady – someone who feeds stray cats in Kaka'ako

Robert Shilling – a developer

Clare Song – the Head of a forensic investigation lab

Stan Takahashi – a Honolulu Police Detective

Malahini (newcomer to Hawai'i) Dictionary

Diamond Head – A famous landmark, and used to mean "to the east" of downtown

Ewa – Generally used to mean "to the west" if you live east of Pearl Harbor

Great Mahele – First formal, western-style, division of lands and property – 1848

Hanai – to be adopted

Haole – a foreigner, or outsider, or Caucasian. Sometimes used pejoratively by locals.

Mana – spiritual power

Kama'aina – Born, or lived a long time, in Hawai'i

Kaka'ako – Semi-industrial area on the ocean side of downtown Honolulu

Kalihi – Older, generally poorer, section of Honolulu

Kawaiahao Church – Oldest permanent church on Oahu, started by missionaries

Koa – Indigenous tree, valued in wood making for its beautiful grains

Magic Island – Not an island, but a man-made peninsula/park near Waikiki

Makai – towards the sea

Mauka – towards the mountains

Pono – righteous, correct, ethical, moral, culturally appropriate Pule - prayer

Pupus – substantial side dishes, finger foods, snacks, etc.

Wahine - woman

PROLOGUE

....

PAPER IS PRECIOUS

Welcome to Old Honolulu
Honolulu, 1880.

Kawika opened his koa wood box, a precious gift from an auntie of David Malo. In it he looked at what he knew were special papers with mana - spiritual power. There was a letter from

Malo to William Richards, a close advisor to King Kamehameha III. He read it out loud to himself, even though he wasn't quite sure of its full meaning:

> I believe it best that at this time, the people should own lands as they do in foreign lands; they work all the harder knowing they own the land, and very likely it is the reason why they love their country, and why they do not go to other places and perhaps that is the reason why they are great farmers.

Kawika knew of and respected Malo, one of the most important Hawai'ian historians. *If he said it, must be true. These were words of wisdom, he thought.*

The second document was a copy of a page ripped out of a report. It was dated March 1855, and was from the final report of the official Land Commission that had decided all the ownership

....

of land resulting from the Mahele, the official division of lands in accordance with foreign laws, and especially the awarding of fee titles to Hawai'ian commoners. It read in part:

> **"But perhaps the greatest benefit that has resulted from the labors of the Commission, coupled with the liberality of our late Sovereign, is the securing to the common people their Kuleana in fee simple; thus raising them at once from a condition little better that that of serfs or mere tenants at will of the Konohikis, to the position of absolute owners of the soul..."**

The words "absolute owners" had been underlined in dark pencil.

"Now this is important, Kawika," his cousin Kimo had emphasized 20 years ago, when they were young. "If someone tells you that you don't own the land, show them this paper. Too many of our people have lost their land because they just cannot understand the haole ways. They lose hope. This is for your protection."

Kawika then picked up the most precious paper of all. It was written all in Hawai'ian. "This is for you and your ohana and for all the generations to come. This is for them long after you and I are gone. Keep it safe. Hide it from the taxman, the lawyers, the haole big shots. This you keep forever."

Now it was 1880. Kawika was an old man, in his sixties. He was not feeling good, with aches and pains in his stomach and back. He needed to find a good place to protect the papers, just in case he would not live much longer. He put them all carefully and neatly into the koa wood box with the polished scrimshaw design on the top. He smiled when he looked at the koa box and especially at the scrimshaw. He thought back to when he got it.

He was just a little kid back then. Whenever his uncle came into Honolulu Harbor on a ship, he would go down to see him. Like his uncle, he loved the ocean from the time for as long as he could remember. His mother said he could swim before he could walk and a two or three mile swim was just like skipping down the street.

Uncle Jonah told him tales of when Lahaina and Hawai'i were the whaling capitals of the world. He told him tales of adventure and shipmates, and even at times crazy, even mad, sea captains. He said ship owners and captains liked having their local sailors whenever they could hire them. This was quite often, if only because western – haole – sailors were always jumping ship whenever they came to islands in the Pacific. They hadn't seen women in months and native girls were always beautiful and you know---exciting. There were times when a ship could have a majority of Kanakas as the crew.

Hawai'ians had sailing in the blood. Uncle Jonah was always fond of telling Kawika: "You come from a people who were the best sailors in the world. Don't ever let anyone tell you it was the Vikings or the Phoencians or haoles like Columbus and Magellen. No! We were the best. We used the stars. When all of the other people of the world stopped sailing for adventure and curiosity, we kept going. When they began farming and sailing only cause it was business, we Hawai'ian still follow the stars and wonder where we can go to next."

"Well, Hawai'i was the last stop on this great adventure. There were no more places to go to, Kawika. But you know, I like to think that it hasn't ended here, here in Hawai'i -nei. We are only the last stop here on this planet we call Earth. But maybe someday we can even go out there. He pointed to the stars. Auwe! I won't be around. Who knows maybe you, maybe someone else from our family? But I hope that when that ship goes out to the stars that there will be a Hawai'ian on board. You gotta have a Hawai'ian, you know. It just seems right. Yeah!"

It was pitch dark on a moonless night as he made his way through a dirt covered side street. He slipped unnoticed through an old cemetery, and worked his way along a tall coral rock wall. Crouching, he jiggled a loose coral rock near the bottom. Looking again to see if anyone was watching, he placed the box behind the loose rock then returned stones to cover it up. He smiled to himself, as he checked to make sure that there was no evidence of it being disturbed.

Kawika then made his way towards Diamond Head. He passed the rice paddy that some Chinaman had planted in the swampy

Moiliili section of town, just above Waikiki. "*I don't know. I can't imagine Hawai'ians going give up poi for a bowl of rice. But rice is ono*", he admitted to himself.

As he got closer to Diamond Head, he then went 'makai' - towards the ocean. He preferred walking this way since so much of Waikiki was swampland and smelled of stagnant water. But since the haoles didn't much care for it, a lot of Hawai'ians still lived there in traditional grass huts.

Spotting the familiar Hawai'ian hut, he knocked on the wooden door. A young Hawai'ian boy greeted him, telling him his father was not at home. The old man gives him a letter. He tells the boy to give it to his dad, who is his brother. The boy promises to do so. Kawika tells him to tell his brother it is those most important papers he has ever had, and that the boy's dad would know what to do. The boy says his dad has been out fishing, but is several days late into port. The boy cannot hide that he is worried that last week's storm might have something to do with it.

"*Don't lose that paper,*" said Kawika firmly.

Chapter 1

THE HEARING

Wednesday, June 15, 2011

The room was smaller than she expected. There was a long wooden straight panel desk with five leather swivel chairs for the Kaka'ako Commissioners. An eight-foot folding table at the end was for staff. Just 25 fold up chairs for the public. Zoe Lee took a seat at the end of the front row, ensuring she could clearly see and hear everyone and everything said – or perhaps whispered. It was 9 a.m. – a time when most working people could never attend a hearing.

Zoe Lee was a young, smart, energetic child of the aina – the land of Hawai'i. She went to journalism school, but only three years after graduation she was the only one in her class still working in the field. At 22, she landed a job on the mainland and won an award for her work. But she always wanted to return home. At 26, somewhat of a celebrity, she surprised everyone by rejecting the mainstream media and taking a job at the *Manoa Investigator.*

The Manoa Investigator was a newly created weekly, financed mostly from an endowment created by one of Hawai'i's 19th century success stories. Whaling mogul, Mij Nohs, had come to Hawai'i first in the 1860's at the height of the whaling frenzy. His son, Bjorn

Nohs, had taken his inheritance and bought prime waterfront properties in Honolulu harbor. From warehouses and ship repairs, the descendants of Nohs lavishly endowed the University of Hawai'i in territorial days, and then after statehood. Bonnie Nohs-Freeman, a grateful graduate of the University of Hawai'i at Manoa, built The Nohs School of Journalism and Government Affairs on the campus during the 1990s, one of the most stunning and modern structures on the campus.

Bonnie was a member of any and all prestigious boards, but she never married. When she died in 2002, without an heir, her considerable fortune was transferred to an estate, headed by a distant nephew. The nephew, Tommy Wong, had gone to Stanford, and founded a high tech firm in Silicon Valley, which added to the family fortune. As director of the Nohs Estate, Tommy was a frequent part-time resident of the Islands, and took an interest in politics. He was often disappointed at the level of public knowledge about government, society, and what we might call civic literacy.

In honor of his Auntie Bonnie, he took a major part of the Estate's endowment and created an alternative to the mainstream media – *The Manoa Investigator. The Manoa*, as it was generally referred to, was different. It initially hired only recent graduates from respected schools of journalism – to provide real jobs for those interested in the field. He paid them the average salary of a public school teacher – so they would be grounded in the economic mainstream, and develop an understanding of the general economic life of the community. He did one other thing to make working at the paper attractive: if you worked at the paper for ten or more years, he would provide you and your immediate family with free health care for the rest of your life.

From when she first heard about it, Zoe knew she wanted to return to work for *The Manoa*. She interviewed twice before being accepted. It wasn't because she needed to prove herself. It was, oddly, that she was almost too experienced for their philosophy. The first year for all new cub reporters was a probationary period, where everyone had to produce a daily blog covering some aspect of Island life, and at least one monthly investigative article. It was a practical training ground for reporters. Tommy hired an experienced and respected editor from the Washington Post, Rachael Jones, paid her handsomely, and told her: "Make *The Manoa* into the most attractive job a journalist could put on their resume."

Jones did, and she was particularly lucky to stumble across Zoe Lee. In no time at all, Zoe's reports were among the best and most widely read on the Higher Education Beat. Later, she was assigned to the Hawai'ian Affairs desk, one of the challenging and thankless assignments you could get. She even took a night course from the Cook Museum director, Dayton Apo.

The light industrial low-rise district of Kaka'ako Honolulu was undergoing an intense and aggressive spurt of high-rise development. Modest walk-up apartments and repair shops were being replaced with luxury condos. Construction sites were frequently halted when ancient Hawai'ian burial remains were discovered. There was a growing tension between a fading 19th century Hawai'ian community, a worn and shabby 20th century afterthought of greasy car engine pits and blue collar bars, and the creation of a new, and modern, 21st century part of the city.

Zoe was covering the hearing, more as a way of getting up to speed on the developments and the Commission than for any particular agenda item.

They are late, she thought, as if the Commissioners wanted to remind the public who was important, whose time was valuable, and whose was not. She doodled on her narrow notebook, and let herself nurture small thoughts of resentment at how those in power took themselves too seriously.

Also in attendance was a well-dressed professional in the typical Aloha shirt and slacks – the uniform of the downtown Bishop Street bankers and corporate executives. Next to him, in the front row, was an attorney – had to be – with a suit and tie and briefcase. They were having a private conversation she could not hear.

In the middle row was an aging, slightly overweight haole couple who looked very nervous and uncomfortable. They were decked out in aloha shirts and old style puka shell necklaces. *Remind me of those tavern owners in Les Mis*, she thought.

In the back was a pretty cool looking young, twenty- something guy, with his own pile of papers, who was obviously closely following the agenda and perhaps was going to present testimony. Zoe had been briefly introduced to him at a party once, but she doubted he remembered her.

Next to him was a middle-aged University of Hawai'i professor, Jon Miller. Zoe once took a Hawai'ian history class from him – it was a class of 100 freshmen – not as impersonal as the mob of 400 that once met in the old Varsity Theater just down the hill from the UH Manoa campus – but still big enough to be lost in the crowd. Most students never had direct contact with the profs, mostly just the teaching assistants. But Zoe Lee had made the effort to meet with Miller a few times, and he inspired her with his knowledge and passion.

Also in the back was a casually dressed Japanese guy with a graying goatee, who seemed to be taking it all in.

Five Commissioners filed in, each with their own wooden nameplate. A laptop computer for each - *you can never tell if they are reading testimony or shopping on line*, she thought. One of the secretarial assistants ensuring commissioners have their folders and their coffee was a young woman – Sheri Iwamoto – a former classmate of Zoe's. They nodded to each other.

The chief of staff for the Commission came in and sat down. His nameplate read Mr. Leighton Thomas. As the Kaka'ako Commission ground through its initial agenda items of administrivia – review of the minutes, corrections noted, approval of the minutes, announcement of the next meeting dates – Yoshiro "Moto" Fujimoto stroked his goatee, and was visibly enjoying his favorite pastime – observing people and guessing their life stories.

Moto came because his Izakawa eatery was located in Kaka'ako, but also because of rumors of gambling operations in the area. He recognized Robert Shilling the developer, and Joe and Molly "Mai Tai" Davis. He also knew of Professor Miller. The young woman in

The Case of the Good Deed

the front, and the young man next to Miller, he had never seen before. Next to the Mai Tai's were Detective Stan Takahashi. Also in the back row was an aging woman in shaggy used clothes. On her lap was a kitten that she affectionately stroked. Fujimoto caught her eye and nodded. She winked at him mischievously.

Leighton Thomas reported on crime statistics and on increased number of arrests for gambling in the area. He also was first to present testimony on the major agenda for the day, a zoning proposal that would convert light industrial to high rise dense urban – which would raise the height limit from 40 feet to 400 feet on a prime lot in the middle of the district. Thomas covered all the nuts and bolts, provided a tax map key, saw no major environmental impacts, and recommended approval.

Just like that, thought Zoe Lee. *Just a matter of fact - tenfold increase in height and density. Not a peep about the environment, lines of sight, or possible Hawai'ian burials. Unbelievable.*

Next up was the attorney. "Good Morning Chair Carleton, members of the Commission. My name is Allison West, III, of Saito Hamilton and Agbayani, representing the interests of Shilling and Associates. I will not read all of my prepared testimony, but would like to highlight some of its most important points. We are in support of the re-zoning proposal. We hereby disclose we do have financial interests in the area. Should the zoning be approved, we will be coming in for permits. By way of demonstrating the kinds of dynamic improvements the zoning will bring, we have included for your review our preliminary engineering renderings, and a private, preliminary environmental assessment, which as you heard from your staff, is consistent with their findings that the zoning per se will not require a full Environmental Impact Statement."

"We would like to note that an independent estimate by a Bank of Waikiki economist is that, if the zoning is approved and we receive all the necessary permits, our future project alone will generate some 400 temporary jobs during construction, 250 permanent jobs once completed, and some $4.5 million in property taxes during the first three years. Shilling and Associates is an established, local – kama'aina firm, known for responsible and culturally sensitive economic development. It is time to recognize that like any other City, Honolulu should maximize the opportunities of prime urban lands. I'll be glad to answer any questions. Thank you for the opportunity to testify."

Son of a bitch, said Zoe under her breath. Of course, the posted agenda on line did not include digital copies of either the staff report or early testimony. All the details, both good and not so good, were buried, hidden, and inaccessible. It would take hundreds of dollars to ask staff to copy the documents after the fact, or a more lengthy freedom of information request. She thought of her poor friend Sheri, who had to depend on these jerks for a low paying job. *If it ain't on line, the public's blind*, her editor would say.

Son of a bitch, thought Moto. If this zoning and projects like the one pushed by Shilling is on up and up, why need hide the details? Shilling on too high a horse. Awful confident.

Before anyone else was called, the cool young guy came up and sat down next to Zoe. "You are Zoe Lee, the reporter right? I'm Kirk Daniels. I work for the Cook Museum. I thought you might like a copy of my testimony. It's kind of long, but it has a lot of good background and detail."

He's got blue eyes, she thought. *She's got a great smile, to go with everything else*, he thought. "Would you have any time for coffee after the hearing, I'm sure there are lots of questions I'll have," she offered.

"Great. How about the Kup a Kaka'ako over on Queen Street? Shall we say 11ish? They serve sandwiches too."

"Joseph Davis," intoned Thomas. Joe shuffled nervously up to the small desk with a microphone set up for public testimony. He fidgeted with the flexible microphone, tapping it with his finger, delaying the inevitable. "Ahem. Can you hear me?"

"Please proceed," said the Chair, not looking up but staring intently at his computer.

Joe removed a crinkled piece of paper from his shirt pocket and smoothed it out. "My name is Joseph B. Davis. I live with my wife Molly...." He provided all the trivial details of his address, and the small walk up apartment he owned. "I support the rezoning. Kakaʻako used to be a nice friendly place. But in the last ten years crime has gone up. The neighborhood is noisy with car repairs and foul smells, gambling and loud arguments when the bars close. We need new and cleaner buildings. This project will create jobs, and change our area for the better. Mahalo for letting me testify."

"Thank you Mr. Davis. Mr. Kirk Daniels."

Kirk brought a thick folder of papers and let it drop on the small testifiers' desk, as if to remind everyone he had done his homework.

"Mr. Chairman, Commission Members, I am Kirk Daniels. I am employed at the Cook Museum as a researcher with an emphasis on land use and Native Hawaiʻian rights. However, today I am testifying as a member of 'Love of the Land'."

"One of our concerns relates directly to the location of known, and as yet unknown, burial plots. Another relates to the likelihood of building foundations negatively impacting the coastal water aquifer."

Moto noticed the slight but distinct change in body language between Shilling and his attorney. He also saw Detective Takahashi shift uneasily in his chair.

Kirk Daniels was determined to present all his important data and arguments to the Commission, confident that the more you told them, the better they would decide. He proceeded in a rapid recitation of a blurr of information. He cited a report that recommended the closing of the bars and car repair shops, cleaning up the sites with Federal funds, and relocating sacred Hawaiʻian bones.

*Oh you poor boy, don't you know that Hawaiʻi style is not to overwhelm with details...*thought Zoe with obvious sympathy on her young face. She admired what he was trying to do, but knew it would not change the outcome.

Daniels repeatedly referred the Commissioners to this and that appendix. A few dutifully flipped to the back of his written testimony, and appeared to be studying the various charts and surveys. The Commissioners were indifferent and tolerant until Daniels departed from his prepared remarks to comment on the politics of development. "Look around this room? The sharks have gathered. Mr. Chairman, we can only imagine that if you approve this zoning, small landowners will be approached to sell out. The rich and powerful will buy up the land, consolidate the parcels. This is all about greed. They've been secretly plotting and planning for years. This is all about sucking the life and the values out of Honolulu with no thought about public good."

Finally, the Chairman interrupted. "Mr. Daniels. We appreciate your detailed and thoughtful testimony. We have written copies. I for one have read it before this hearing. Could you summarize and wrap it up?"

Daniels stopped abruptly. "Thank you Mr. Chairman." "Professor Jon Miller," said Thomas without thanking Daniels. Jon Miller, Ph.D., was a well-known and admired professor of Hawai'ian history. His books and articles were used and quoted widely. He was also more than an academic, for he often testified at public meetings. He was a fixture down at the legislature. Zoe credited him with inspiring her to become an investigative journalist.

Attorney Viper began taking careful notes. Miller's reputation and knowledge of traditional Hawai'ian land holdings could not be easily dismissed.

"This may seem a straightforward policy decision about the future of Kaka'ako," he began. But if you look closer, and deeper, you may find it is more complicated."

"First, there is the issue of historical justice and original titles to various land parcels. We all know what happened during King Kamehameha III's reign, when private land ownership was institutionalized and imposed on a culture and Nation with very different ideas about land and resources. Over the last thirty-five years alone, fifty-five ownership claims have been successfully challenged in court. This is due in part to the access to Royal deeds and ownership records through excellent translations from the original Hawai'ian. Genealogy research has connected Hawai'ian

The Case of the Good Deed

family land rights to current residents. Thus, I recommend a thorough review of 19th century historical land transactions to ensure that the ownership is not in doubt."

Moto need to talk to this smart man some time, Fujimoto thought to himself.

"Second, recent construction has revealed that major sections of the district were common burial grounds back when Honolulu was just developing as a small city. I recommend that representatives of the Hawai'i Burial Investigation Agency be present during all preliminary site preparation. With more research, we should be closing down some of these outdated bars and car shops out of respect for the historical burials we will most surely find."

"And third, a recent Tourism Promotion Board survey of visitors had a little noticed pattern of responses when asked what tourists most cherished about Honolulu. It was not the fancy hotels, although they were praised. It was not just the food, as delicious as it could be. It was the experience of being at Ala Moana Park and Magic Island and looking not only towards the ocean but also towards the beauty of the mountains. They love looking up at the tall, verdant green hills, perhaps with rain clouds and rainbows. So one important consideration might be that allowing a wall of condos on the mauka – the mountain side - of the coast might not be the best way to enhance the visitor experience. Thank you for the opportunity to testify."

The Chair thanked Miller and then abruptly took a 'short' recess. Zoe suspected this was to encourage members of the public to leave and return to their busy lives, and not be there to witness the actual voting. The Davis couple, the lady with the kitten, the Detective, and his friend left. After thirty minutes, during which Moto observed Leighton Thomas being very chummy with Shilling and his lawyer, they returned.

The motion to approve was moved, seconded and unanimously endorsed in a flash, with one amendment. Future applicants would be required to pay for a private, independent assessment of possible Hawai'ian burials on their site. The gavel came down. The hearing was over.

Zoe Lee was not naïve. She had seen this before, where it seemed that no matter what compelling testimony was presented, it was as if minds were already made up. Kirk came over and sat down. He thought he knew what she was thinking. "Don't be surprised. This is just round one. Predictable. If they don't approve zoning at this stage I've seen them taken to court. The game is not lost," he said to console her.

"Kirk, okay to call you Kirk? I am well aware how many of these hearings go. I go to them all the time. I understand how zoning triggers a feeding frenzy. So you have some good information for me? Let's go get that coffee."

BIG CHANGES COMING TO KAKA'AKO.

Submitted by Zoe Lee

The Kaka'ako Commission voted unanimously yesterday to rezone five acres of prime light industrial land to high density urban. The decision will raise the height limits to 450 feet. Testifying in favor of the re-zoning were several individuals representing private developers and property owners that could, potentially, reap huge profits. Robert Shilling, known for his outspoken prodevelopment views, said the re-zoning would "pave the way for a revitalization of a new city within the city."

Opposed to the action were University of Hawai'i Professor Jon Miller, and a spokesperson for Love of the Land. Miller raised the issues of possible original land titles, and the probable existence of ancient burial grounds

Kirk Daniels, representing Love of the Land, presented previous studies and planning documents calling for a more thoughtful way to clean up the area. The Executive Director, Mr. Leighton Thomas said, "Actually, today's decision means nothing. Anyone wanting to build under the new zoning will still need to submit plans, secure free title to parcels, and receive building permits. This is just a way to begin the conversation," he explained. "And it's not like we are changing everything. Some of the small industrial uses and the blue collar bars can stay."

Tomorrow: Who owns what in Kaka'ako?

Chapter 2

THE WALL

Thursday, December 1, 2011

Henry Doyle had been driving a city bus for ten years. At age 34, he was one of the veterans, knew Honolulu inside and out, and enjoyed his work. He knew the streets, but he also knew where to drink and where to gamble. As he drove the bus down Punchbowl Street, he passed the State Capitol on the right, and then City Hall on the left. But he saw neither. He was distracted. His live-in girlfriend was giving him grief over his drinking and gambling with the boys and threatening to leave him.

His smartphone pinged in his pocket, telling him there was a text message. It was against the rules to even have his personal phone on the bus, let alone try to answer it or read a text. He didn't care. If this was from Trish, he needed to see it.

He glanced down at the phone just as he was turning left onto South King Street. "Oh shit, she's pissed again..." He didn't finish his thought as he looked up just in time to see his bus plow into the three foot archaic lava stone wall in front of the iconic Kawaiahao Church – the oldest in Honolulu. The slow crunching and scraping as he slammed on the breaks seemed to hit him as the sound of his own job being obliterated.

Henry could hardly believe his eyes…here was his bus, with a half dozen passengers, sticking through one of the most important cultural sites in the Islands. He cursed Trish again, all the more since he knew it was his fault. He picked up the official radio and painfully called his supervisor, then the police.

***

It took Detective Stan Takahashi twenty minutes before he arrived at the scene. His car partly blocked one lane of Punchbowl, but he didn't care. Already there was an ambulance with EMTs checking out the passengers. The bus driver, identified as a Henry Doyle, aged 34, was sitting on the curb with his head in his hands, obviously distraught.

Takahashi pulled out his notebook, and took Doyle's statement, then wandered over to the partly crumpled wall, which had also spilled out onto the sidewalk. He knew Henry, having seen him at one or two underground poker rooms, the kind that attracted an occasional police officer who saw nothing wrong with a little innocent wagering on cards.

His eye was drawn to something brown under the crushed lava stones – a box of some kind. He put on his "evidence gloves" and picked up the wooden box, which seemed to have been made of koa wood, one of Hawai'i 's native trees, and prized for its attractive grain. It was locked. He shook it, and heard something shift inside. It might be an important find, apparently placed inside the wall a long time ago.

But Stan was not thinking about the value of the box per se. He was thinking of who would get credit for finding it – the regular detectives, or that smart ass Special Unit led by that smart ass, know it all Charlie C. Chang, known by his friends and foes just as Charlie C. *No way will I let Charlie C. get his hands on this case. No way is he going to upstage us again. We are the real detectives, the ones who do the work- day in and day out. This is ours. This is mine*, he thought.

He removed the box and casually walked over to his car. Inside he dialed an old friend and classmate, now the Director of the world-renowned Cook Museum.

"Dr. Apo here." "Dayton. Stan."

"Hey Stanley. Howzit."

"Pretty good. You know how it is. How is my niece doin up there?"

"She's a good worker. We have her doing inventory for the Museum now. Glad to give her a chance to get work experience. How can I help you today my friend?"

"Need a favor, Dayton. There has been one crazy bus accident where a city bus plowed into the wall by Kawaiahao Church."

"Oh no!!! This is bad news. The history…the heritage. How bad was it damaged?"

"Looks bout ten feet will need to be replaced. Lots of crumbly coral rock. I suspect you guys at Cook Museum will be called in to help ensure it gets done right."

"Yes, I'm sure we can help."

"There's more, and this needs to be just between you and me. Found one old box that fell out of the friggin wall. It is locked, and considering where it came from, I'd like you and your guys to take a look at it and find out if it is valuable, you know, or historic or something li dat."

"Sure, sure, no problem. Where can I get it? I know - my hyper eager pain in the neck young researcher Daniels. I need to give him something to do before he pokes his nose into where it doesn't belong. I'll give him the box. I'll instruct him that this is highly sensitive and he should tell no one."

"Mahalo Dayton. I owe you one."

"Well, got any tickets to the UH game this Saturday?"

"I'll see what I can do."

"Mahalo Plenty. Talk to you soon."

Chapter 3

IT'S ALL ABOUT WHO YOU KNOW

Friday, December 2, 2011

Takahashi was driving up to the Cook Museum. He had not seen Apo in about a year. It was always profitable when he did. The director never asked questions about what was that word—provenance - of anything he had brought up to the museum.

And hell if I would know, he said to himself. *Doc's the expert.*

He thought back of their long friendship. It started out playing sports here. They were both on the same Little League baseball teams. Doc could hit as well as pitch. We took a couple of state titles. Lost out in the nationals, but hey they had good teams from all over back then, even the ones from Asia.

Though they went to separate schools---young Takahashi or "Taka" in the public school system and Apo in the fabled Kamehameha Schools. "It's Kamehameha School, not Kam. You better get it right!" Doc would often demand of all the public school kids.

Of course, they played on opposite teams. The two played football and baseball. Since different scholastic leagues were involved, they would only occasionally play in pre-season games. The could have, if his alma mater had been good enough, played against each other in the State Championships, but in all the years that Taka played ball his team never made to the State playoffs in either sport.

Doc, on the other hand, always got to play in the state finals in each of his high school years at Kamehameha. And one year they even took the State Championship in baseball. Though Doc played football in college on the mainland he became more oriented towards academics, not that he would have been drafted by any professional team, but Apo went on to get advanced degrees including his dual doctorate in anthropology and archaeology. From there, he went on to work at some of the best museums in the world and returned to Hawai'i to become the director of the world famous Cook Museum.

You had to hand it to Doc, thought Takaahashi. *Even back then in Little League, he made his prediction. It was after a game at Laniakila Field. Doc boasted that someday he would be the director of the Museum. Located just a few blocks from where they had just played a game.*

Apo came back still looking fit and athletic, tall and smooth talking. He was cultured. Good-looking, he could charm women of all ages. They said he raised a lot of money by playing up to the rich widows and wives in Hawai'i. They all loved him.

When he and Apo were having a Hawai'ian lunch at one of the famous Hawai'ian food restaurants near the Museum, he asked Apo why he didn't get married. "Hey, Taka, I have an obligation to spread my aloha to all the women. It's a tough job, but it's gotta be done. And besides, Taka, how many times you been married already?" That always ended that conversation.

Takahashi was at the Museum in another five minutes. After parking, he went straight into the director's office. He had wanted to get more background on the Church and the damage to the wall.

Dr. Dayton Apo said he saw that when the city bus hit the stone wall it tore into the foundation and left small boulders and big pieces of coral all over the sidewalk and into the side yard of the sacred Kawaiahao Church. Beyond the pile of rubble there were cracks and fissures in the wall fronting King Street that stretched for another twenty or thirty feet in several directions.

"When it was built over a hundred years ago, I understand," said Officer Takahashi to Dr. Apo, a highly regarded archaeologist, "it wasn't that solid to begin with, since coral tends to be porous and becomes more brittle as it ages, more than other types of rock and concrete."

Apo pulled out a document from his desk. "This is the 1978 application to put Kawaiahao on the National Register of Historical Places. Here's what it says about the wall:

The 6 foot high coral block wall was erected around the church site, ca. 1875, was reduced to 2 feet in 1899 to avoid repetition of the Wilcox revolution of 1889, when Honolulu Rifles fortified themselves on the church grounds and commanded the makai portion of the Palace grounds. Walls on the King Street (mauka) and right (ewa) sides consist of natural coral rock in random sizes set in heavy mortar joints which average 3"- 4" thick in the horizontal and 4"- 8" wide vertically. The rear (makai) and left (Waikiki) walls are finished smooth in modern white cement stucco over the coral rock....and in 1925 the outer walls were spray-coated with a cement plaster to preserve the coral blocks from damage by birds pecking at them.

"No wonder it crumbled so easily, even the birds were at it. And that's what made it easier on the passengers," he continued. "There were no injuries. Everyone, especially the old tutus – the seniors - were just shaken up a little. There was one old lady who was adamant about future bus rides. She said that she would never ride with that driver, Henry. Then she added: 'And you wait til I see your mother at church next Sunday. You going get it from me. I going let her know. Going be jus' like she was on the bus seat next to me. She going gat scared like you wen make me! In fact my heart still going BOM! BOM! BOM!... BOM BOM! AUWE!'"

"I suppose," said Apo, "that the driver will never drive again for the city. Well maybe not. The union will fight for his job, but the City will find a way to fire him. It seems that it's an easy turn to make for bus drivers, providing that you pay attention and drive carefully. Don't blame the old tutu for yelling at the driver."

Takahashi said the driver was quite broken up about it. "He was worried for his job and his career. He kept saying over and over about how it was all his girlfriend's fault. If she hadn't called him while he was driving all of this would never have happened. To which I responded, that I wouldn't talk so much since I would have to write it down and his employer will, of course, ask for the police report in figuring out the punishment for him. This wouldn't look good for him. I asked him if his bosses let you folks use cell phones while driving. He shut up immediately."

"I told the bus driver–"Henry you should just accept responsibility for the accident and hope your union can get you out. Then I won't have to write down about your girlfriend's call and how distracted you were. Who knows maybe just a suspension and they'll send you to remedial driving classes."

Apo noted that the wall came up after the church, and had been repaired on several occasions. For all anyone knew, it was during one of the repairs that someone slipped in the box for one reason or another. It would not have been an official act of the church, since that was not their practice. Valuables were kept in the basement lockers.

Apo mentioned the box and assigning it to his young researcher. "I'll supervise him, of course." "Look Kirk. I want you to clean the outside of this box a little bit. Then carefully open it up. I trust you won't gouge the wood like you did the last time. This will be good practice for you," he told him.

"So Dayton, you know that box I gave you, it is kind of evidence if someone finds out about it. So now it is just between you and me and my staff. Just got to make sure you don't lose it or anything. And if it turns out to be important, well, you'll let me know, right?"

"No problem Taka. If it is valuable or important, I'll let you know right away. Probably nothing. But the important thing is that the Museum be, you know, considered, if there is going to be a contract to evaluate and rebuild the wall, if you get my drift. I imagine it could be an important contract, as in several hundred thou."

"Don't worry. I have a friend over at the Historic Preservation Office who probably would be involved. I don't think it would be a problem for them to consider the most knowledgeable Museum in the state to handle it.

"Preciate it Taka. Preciate it."

The bus incident was well covered by the media, including pictures of the broken wall.

***

It was 6:00 pm. and Kirk was in his small museum office trying to finish up several assignments he'd gotten from Dr. Apo the day before. *Dammit! He always gives me these last minute, got to be done ASAP assignments. Well, I've had it. I'm going,* he said to himself.

As he started to leave, he picked up the dirty wooden box. *Since the police are involved, I'm sure he promised them something soon. So I'm the last guy here, he thought. It's time to go and I'll just take it home and work on it tonight or tomorrow morning.*

He put down his backpack and carefully removed the box. It was old, but well made. After carefully and respectfully examining it, he wrapped it in a newspaper, and stuffed it in his backpack. He then got on his bike, and began the 30-minute trip to his rental unit in Palolo Valley.

Back home, after a shower and an old ham sandwich, he pulled out the box. He looked for, and found, a simple razor cutter. Well here goes. He made a few quick strong strokes. Crack! It wasn't that loud a sound, but to Kirk it seemed to reverberate throughout his small apartment.

Later that evening, Apo got a text message from Kirk. He had taken the box home and was able to open it. He found some pieces of paper, some in English but one completely in Hawai'ian, including the word he knew a little about: Mahele. He said he would be going to the University tomorrow do more research. It was one of his regular graduate class days anyhow. He also said he found a few letters with correspondence in a pidgin English. They didn't seem important but he would skan in the papers for Apo to see.

Kirk could imagine how Apo would have responded in a loud and angry tone: *Kirk! You were just to open this box and that's it. Can't follow the simplest instructions. You're one typical mainlander always believing they know more than the natives.*

Chapter 4

MAGIC ISLAND

Friday Afternoon, December 2, 2011

Charlie C. Chang pulled his vintage silver DeLorean into the Magic Island parking lot. He was proud of this unique second hand car, which featured gull-wing doors, an innovative fiberglass chassis and underbody structure, along with a brushed stainless steel body. The car became widely known and iconic for its appearance as the time machine in the *Back to the Future* film trilogy. The company went out of business in 1983. There were only some 6,000 known to exist – but who really knew how many were left. Charlie's was the only one in Hawai'i, bought three years ago. At age 62, Charlie felt no guilt in this indulgence. "Wat, you having a mid- life crisis? Taking a mistress? Men and their toys..." his sister had scolded him.

Magic Island was one of his favorite places on Oahu – next to the sweeping Ala Moana beach, a small swimming pool protected by a stone breakwater, and stunning views of Diamond Head, the Kookau Mountains, and the rapidly developing industrial area of Kaka'ako.

His uncle Tony had been deeply involved in preventing the 1964 man-made peninsula from becoming a high rise resort complex, and keeping it as a park. It was the perfect meeting place of locals, visitors, joggers, newlyweds, and anyone who enjoyed the beauty of a Honolulu sunset.

He turned off the engine and waited, admiring the growing canopy of monkey pod, Tacoma, and shower trees. On the Diamond Head side of the parking lot, there were three stretch limos serving Japanese wedding couples, who were being escorted by photographers to the most picturesque spots. The brides were often in traditional flowing white gowns, accompanied by skinny, awkward grooms trying to look confident in their tuxedos or silk wedding suits.

Everyone else was in shorts. Because it was December, small groups of determined runners circled the park, preparing for the upcoming Honolulu Marathon. Older couples, walking their dogs and grandchildren gave them a wide berth. The smell of barbecue meats on small hibachi cookers drifted in the air.

After ten minutes, the man Charlie came to meet pulled up in a thirty year-old yellow Datsun station wagon. Charlie glanced through his dark sunglasses at the shaggy haired, Japanese-American driver. An observer would not be able to tell if these two were part of an illicit drug deal, or completely unrelated.

Chang waited, glancing around to ensure no one was watching… then slowly got out of the car wearing a University of Hawai'i cap, a faded Honolulu Marathon finisher tee shirt, shorts and flipflops. He was anything but a detective leading an elite investigations unit.

The Datsun driver let Charlie stroll over to the Ala Moana beach side of the park, then casually joined him under a Tacoma tree. His name was Yoshiro "Moto" Fujimoto, aged 50, but looking older with his graying goatee. His nickname – "Moto" was, one rumor went, given to him because he reminded his first supervisor of the 30's fictional character, Mr. Moto – although he never could see the connection. Actually, it was short for Fujimoto. Born in Japan, he immigrated in his 20s to Hawai'i, did well in school, and spent 10 years first as a full-time taxi driver, then as a part-time Aikido instructor to youth offenders and police recruits. Both experiences taught him to be a keen observer of people, their personalities, and nonverbal communication. He also worked with homeless people in the urban areas. It was through these encounters that he came to know Charlie and other police officers. Charlie took Aikido lessons from him, and they shared a love of food. He now quietly and anonymously ran a local Izakaya restaurant in Honolulu's Kaka'ako district – Toronaga's – named after his favorite character in the novel Shogun, and based on the reputed life of Tokugawa.

"I never get tired of this place, Moto," said Charlie.

"Trees bigger and nicer these days, but building cranes and high rises ruin view," countered Fujimoto. With that brief exchange, Charlie and Moto strode off at a brisk pace heading toward the Diamond Head side. For several minutes neither spoke, as they took in the Friday evening Magic Island crowd. Sailboats were coming and going. A few surfers were getting the last waves. Due to some much needed winter rains, Diamond Head was green. They counted three wedding couples, and walked past a large rental tent set up for a picnic sponsored by an evangelical church. Strollers and walkers led tiny and midsized dogs, and young mothers jogged by pushing baby carriages. Every possible ethnic face and body type was swarming over this little park.

"How goes soap opera?" asked Fujimoto, referring to the intense internal politics of the Honolulu Police Department.

"The Police Board is under public pressure after the sexual assault scandal, so every unit is anxious to get credit for everything. People who have been good friends for years are starting to distance themselves, hesitate, and get suspicious. Bad vibes."

"Lose trust, lose direction," said Moto. "No 'On,' no "Giri.' Very bad vibes."

Following the untimely death of Charlie's wife two years ago of cancer, Moto had become a frequent companion who shared personal and professional interests. Moto was also a widower, but he had never talked much about the wife he lost ten years before in a car accident.

After circling the park, weaving through the curved sidewalks, by mutual purpose and agreement, they began moving towards the large spreading banyan tree on the southwest corner. Their targets were two aging, slightly overweight figures sitting on foldable chairs under the banyan, facing west, where the sun would set in typical spectacular fashion.

Molly and husband Joe Davis ran a small, seedy walk-up, ten- unit apartment in the middle of the Kaka'ako light industrial district.

Whatever was going on in their neighborhood, Molly and Joe tended to know about it. They enjoyed sneaking in some alcohol to the park, and were pretty good at making mai tais. It became their nickname: "Mai Tai" Molly and Joe.

"I don't know what you see in them, most of what they say is BS", grumbled Moto.

"I know, I know. Just take it all in. They are always working some minor scam, but I've learned to read between the lines. It's what they say, what they don't say. The odd questions they ask, the body language, it is usually worth the conversation. Besides, they always give us a sample of their mai tais!"

On cue, Molly started waving to them to come over, holding up a plastic cup filled with the oh-so-sour, and oh-so-refreshing home brew with good rum.

"Charlie C., Moto-san. Happy Aloha Friday. Join us for a bit. Got some inside dope for ya!!" Shouted Molly.

"Backyard lime tree doing well this year," commented Moto. "What is new in your neighborhood?" asked Charlie as he accepted the cup.

"You know that three story walk up a block from us? Sold out to a developer for big bucks, " mumbled Joe. "Hate to see all those high rises, and hate to see greedy little landowners become millionaires for just sitting on their asses and waiting for somebody to make em an offer."

"Wat, you're jealous," observed Charlie.

"Joey's family has owned our land for years, and nobody ever gave us any kind of offer. We ain't givin up, and we can't stand to see so-called friends sellin out," said Molly.

Fujimoto watched Molly and Joe closely. He was a pretty good read of how body language and the tone of one's voice reflected moods and meanings. There was an edginess in this odd couple today, he thought.

"Heard any good rumors?" asked Charlie.

"Check out the traffic accident reports, particularly in the Capitol area," suggested Joe.

"Thanks for the tip," said Charlie as he and Moto eased their way down the sidewalk.

"Something fishy. Something different," offered Moto, as they passed a young couple going the other way.

***

Like many young couples, Kekoa Potter and Sheri Ishihara found that Magic Island was a cheap date, a pleasant walk, a chance to talk, and a pretty romantic chance to see a sunset. As the sky began to glow red, conversations seemed to stop as many drifted to the western side of the island to see if there was a green flash.

"Kekoa, I can't stop thinking about it. I'm just a lousy entry-level secretary, and if something happens like raising the rent or even knocking down my apartment, I don't know what to do. Like, where can I live? I can't afford anywhere else. My Mom says I'll have to move back to Hilo and help out in the store. I can't stand Hilo. I want to stay here, near you."

"Look Sheri, don worry so much. Din't I jus get a job teaching preschool nearby? Preschool is a big ting these days. It's goin to expand, you wait and see. I'll be able to afford a good apartment, and get you out of that rat hole run by dose greedy landlords. Always scheming, never telling us what is going on. Always drunk. We need to get you outta there. Jus don worry so much."

"I wish I could be so sure. Kekoa, you are my guy, and I'm proud of you, and, well, I want to be with you. I want to start a life with you. But we have to be practical. How can we start a family, have a kid, when we can't afford a decent place to live, and we can't afford to move."

"But I just got this good job."

"Yes, and I'm proud of you, but you know yourself the preschool is attached to a charter school, and charters are struggling to survive. Just last week that Kalihi charter folded. The state doesn't care about charters or preschools. Until you can get a job with the DOE, like I just don't know what we can do. I just don't know." She began to weep quietly.

"Look, I'll talk to Joe and Molly and try to find out how long they are going to keep the apartment. But don't get discouraged, girl."

"Haven't we always found a way? You are my girl, my, like, future wife, I hope, so I'm not gonna let them get us down. You'll see. If Hawai'i is not good for people like us, what is it good for?"

Charlie C., Fujimoto, Joe, Molly, Kekoa and Sheri all gazed at the sunset from wherever they were on Magic Island, but no one saw the fabled green flash.

***

Chapter 5

CHINATOWN

Tuesday, December 13, 2011

Chang was shopping. Usually he went to Chinatown. The dinner fare would more than likely be Chinese. Charlie considered himself an expert - this meant he held himself to be a scholar on the subject and a practitioner who could handle himself in a competition with any wannabe at all of the Chinese restaurants in town. "I'm gonna wok'em" he never tired of boasting. And he was good. Everyone admitted that.

When he went out to eat Chinese food, the owners always made sure their number one chef would prepare his meal as well as those of the company he brought with him. If he didn't think the dishes were up to his standard, he would always say to the owner: Wassa matter? How come I got the no. 3 cook? Think I one tourist or what? It was the practice of some restaurants to let the neophyte cooks serve the tourists: what do they know?

But today he was at The Quixotic, that new supermarket chain store from Japan just at the edge of Chinatown. He was looking for some fresh bok choy, finding the ones in Chinatown to be a little too old and dry. My fault for not going earlier this morning, he chided himself.

"Hows'it Charlie?" A shrill wahine's voice rang out from five aisles away.

"Oh, no! I pray to my ancestors don't let it be......" But it was no use. He turned around and it was Mai Tai Molly and Joe. Molly's family name was Jones, and Joe's was Davis, but everyone called them the Mai Tais. It was never clear if they were ever formally married, although they always claimed to be.

"Wassa matter? You usually buy in Chinatown?"Wassa matter? You usually buy in Chinatown?"

"You usually try to keep it in the family, Charlie", said Joe.

"Not so"said Charlie. "It's cheaper if you know how to buy - fresher. And they have all the ingredients for Chinese cuisine. But as Lao Tzu said, the way to a great meal is a journey through many stops." "Lao Za? Who's that? I thought your mentor was the great detective Charlie Chan."Joe said with a loud laugh, causing his body to shake.

"Shut up Joe! Don't show off your ignorance! Charlie Chan was always quoting Confusion! Remember him in The House without a Key. Hey, you know he stayed in the Moana Surfrider?" said Molly.

"Ah so honorable lady." Charlie made a bow and proceeded with his Warner Oland imitation. "You no doubt refer to the great Chinese philosopher Confucius. And I believe it was the Halekulani – known in a famous novel as The House Without a Key."

"Well whatevas or whoeva!" She said. "So whatcha making? Egg Foey Young?"

"Mrs. Mai Tai, egg foo young is not authentic Chinese cuisine. It was invented in San Francisco for Americans," he said.

"Nah, Charlie, no give me dat. Egg Foo Young is to you pakes what hot dog is to the Americans. They both the real deal."Joe was adamant.

And that's how the conversation went for another five or so minutes. Then Charlie said, "Well, have to go now. So Joe, tell me how much did they offer you for the apartment?" Joe made a scowling face and said, "They only wanted to pay me a million half and I told them....."

"Shut up Joe, this all supposed to be confidential" Mrs. Mai Tai said, as she kicked her husband.

"Aloha amigos. Gotta start cooking." Charlie left with a sly grin on his face as Mrs. Mai Tai kicked Joe again.

***

Chang made a mental note. Molly and Joe had more than a passing interest in Kaka'ako development. His next stop was Julie's Bar, just around the corner from the open market. Chinatown had its vibrant side, but was also becoming seedy, with trash and litter all over the sidewalks. There was not a single block without one or two dirty and smelly homeless men, staring numbly at the pedestrians.

Julie was a third generation bar owner, presiding over a dive with sawdust on the floors, a yellow dimly lit interior, and old tables and chairs that emitted the constant aroma of stale beer. Julie was getting on in years, and tried to cover up her age with thick layers of mascara, heavy face powder, and smudged deep red lipstick. She had a gap in her front upper tooth. Chang did not relish his visits, but Julie seemed to know a lot about what went on in Chinatown, and he needed to cultivate this source.

"Charlie my handsome young man, what bring you to our establishment?" She poured a cup of tea from a teapot on an old hotplate. She knew Charlie's tastes.

"Julie, you know I can't stay away from your high class place, and I've always had a thing for you, you know that."

"Bullshit Charlie, you wan somting, so what you bring Julie to trade, huh?" she said showing her missing front upper teeth.

"Your favorite, fresh apple bananas!"

"North Shore?"

"Course, that's the kine you like, right?"

"Dat all? She said as she peered over the bar at Charlie's plastic bag.

"Almost forgot. The fresh shrimp."

Julie grabbed the plastic bag, shoved her face into it and gave it a noisy sniff. "Ok. Fresh enough. What do you wanna know?

"Been to the open market lately?"

"Every day, 6:30 sharp. You know dat."

"Seen the Mai Tais around?"

"Doze creepy, sleezy mainland haoles? Up to no good always I'd say."

"Just wondering, notice if they are any different these days?"

"Dey use to buy the day old veggies. Now, they go to the fresh booths. Now they buy the good kind sashimi too."

"Preciate it, Julie. Preciate it." He sipped his tea. Looked around the bar at the two very idle men hunkered over a table in the back. He could not understand how Julie managed to keep it going year after year, even with the illegal poker games in the back room.

Charlie strolled out of the bar and headed for his vintage DeLorean parked up the street, hoping none of the stray cats had "marked" his tires again.

Chapter 6

....

THE ACCIDENTAL TOURIST

Wednesday, December 14, 2011

It was still dark when Kirk left his apartment with his bicycle. He was going for his usual morning ride. The sun still had another hour before it would poke its head up at the Waimanalo horizon. Kirk wished he could be there to see it since it was one of the great joys of his life in Hawai'i. But today he was going to bike around Kaka'ako and one of the valleys above the city.

Since he was just a kid of 11, he always got up an hour or so before sunrise. Back then, he would either go biking or running. He loved to run and always made his school's track team. He continued running in college and after graduation. What made Hawai'i his running paradise was the opportunity to go running and biking all year around.

When he was growing up in Michigan, he could run only until December. It got too cold and there was too much snow and mainly ice. He wasn't that crazy. So he still would get up and do some calisthenics indoors and reading, but that was it. His parents laid down the law come December: he was to stay indoors until it got closer to springtime. And that's what he liked best about living in Hawai'i. It was perpetual spring and summer for him.

"Yeah, the local folks would make a big thing about how it would get colder come November and they would say: "You know it going rain plenny more." He would answer: "You don't know cold til it gets below zero, and in fact at least 20 degrees below." It was as if he had come from a foreign land when he talked like that. They would all be puzzled and couldn't really relate. "Of course I saw snow one time. Eh, haole boy, get snow on Mauna Kea, you know." Or, "Yeah, when I went to school in Chicago, I saw snow. I not stupid you know. I seen the white stuff." Or, "I gat sister in Vermont. She always sending pics and the family Christmas card is always her kids with a snowman or riding one sled. We not ignorant here."

It got a little warmer for him when his father decided to move the whole family to Northern California when he was about to start high school. There was a great promotional opportunity for him from the big insurance company he worked for. And so all five of them, his younger brother and sister and parents joined the westward move to California.

The timing couldn't have been more ideal. He was getting his license to drive and now he had the room to drive. Dad couldn't have picked a better place for a kid with a car. True, the first car wasn't much, but it was a classic. His father said his first car was an old style Volkswagen bug, and he said if he had kids, that would be their first car. He knew everything about it and how to fix anything that went wrong. "Bugs last forever if you know how to care for them. And I expect you to hand it down to your brother and sister when they're ready." So he had to learn to care for the bug.

It was worth it in California. Maybe in Michigan, kids would have laughed at him. But here: "Man! You have the classic. They're hard to find now. Only thing better would have been the van!" He became popular early in their move.

What changed his life was something else he discovered in California. The ocean. That was an experience he could never have in the middle of America. True, his values were formed there in the American heartland. The values of thrift, loyalty, honesty, pride of home and country, not trying to stand out but never backing down either. The values of the old Gary Cooper and James Stewart old time Hollywood movies his parents always watched, and which the kids had to watch with them.

The great Pacific Ocean gave something more: surfing. Kirk took to surfing and loved it. He asked for, and his father gave him a schedule of work around their new house, which was an older and needed repairs. If he did any work, the father would pay him for each work assignment. But Kirk would hold the money until he got enough to get a used surfboard.

It was a dinged up board, but it was a Greg Noll board. Sure it cost more, but Kirk knew it would go well with his bug. Two classics brought together. Kirk didn't master surfing like he did running and biking. But he was okay. He knew he wouldn't be a champion, but that was fine with him. He just loved the waves and being out there in the vast, seemingly endless, Pacific Ocean.

He continued surfing off and on through college. Did well in school and, while there, discovered his love of ancient history, and even more: prehistoric civilizations. Archaeology became his love. He was determined to get a doctorate and discover old civilizations, or be able to uncover the mystery of the Mayas or ancient scripts that couldn't be deciphered at first, or be the first to find and enter a tomb of some ancient god, king, or pharaoh.

Then it happened. The crossroads of his life. He had just about finished the work for his masters degree at Southern Cal. The guys he hung out with that last year were also surfers, who hadn't been surfing for a while because of their studies. The group included a kid from Hawai'i who said, "You haven't surfed til you've done the winter surf at Banzai or Waimea Bay."

Of course they all knew that. They hated to be reminded of it. A couple of the group had been to Hawai'i for a week once, and they readily supported that claim. Only Kirk and two others had never surfed there. So they all agreed after the Master's award ceremony, they would be off on the first plane to Hawai'i. And they would surf for a half-year or so. It would be winter surf in the land of paradise.

***

Kirk Daniels made it to Hawai'i. He couldn't believe what a place it was. He loved the ocean, the warmth of the sun, the nights, and the people. He got to like the food, even day old poi. And as a test of his acculturation to the land, he alone among the group of six said, "You know I really like Spam." The others couldn't go beyond loco moko – the hamburger steak on rice, smothered in gravy and topped with a fried, egg – then plenty of ketchup. "Real ono, man!" he would always blurt out.

***

Kirk had been riding his bike for exercise for over an hour. Stopping at a few of his favorite spots. The sun was coming up now since summer was almost here. Well, the Hawai'ian summer. Today would have been summer almost anywhere on the mainland except Florida and Arizona, he thought.

So that's how I got here and decided to stay, he said, reminiscing to himself. I didn't go back with the gang. And I've never looked back. Sure looks like it's going to a great day in paradise, he said to himself. Then he looked to the Koolau mountains. Oops! Spoke too soon---grey clouds - and they seem to be massing. Maybe it might rain later. The weather report a few days ago did say chance of heavy showers later this week. But then you could never believe those reports.

Eh! Who cares? Rain---shine. Still a great day in Hawai'i -nei.

It did not take Kirk Daniels long to dive into Hawai'i history, and its issues. He joined the non-profit advocacy group 'Love of the Land,' and landed a job as a researcher at the renowned Cook Museum. It was back in June when he first met Zoe Lee at a Kaka'ako Commission hearing, and they began dating soon after. As many a mainland transplant, he had seen what neglect had done to the mainland environment, and wanted to do his part to prevent it from happening in Hawai'i. He was a quick study. He started learning Hawai'ian language as well. He took up the ukulele.

It was covering Hawai'ian affairs that connected Zoe Lee to Kirk Daniels, and in no time it was more than a purely professional relationship. Where Zoe was intellectually committed to journalism, Daniels gave her passion for changing society. Where Zoe had taken so much of Hawai'i for granted, as was often the case with those who grew up in the Islands, the Cook Museum researcher opened her eyes to the richness of the host culture - and to so much that was often hidden from large segments of the population. Kirk was often amazed at how different groups lived disconnected to each other in such a small place.

They were both angry at what was happening to Hawai'i, and vowed that if, through her journalism or his research, they could do something about it, they would.

Chapter 7

THE PROF

Friday, December 16, 2011

When Kirk had pried open the box, he'd found several documents. His work at the museum told him the papers were old. He had carefully unfolded them and instantly recognized historical texts from the 19th century, and a rather official looking paper written all in Hawai'ian, with an official stamp, also in Hawai'ian. It would need to be translated, but he could make out some familiar place names that appeared to describe land boundaries. He had seen similar texts in the Mahele Book.

Kirk and Zoe scheduled their meeting with Professor Jon Miller at 3:30, in the UH history department – nicknamed Fantasy Hall by former graduate students poking fun at some of the professors who they believed were living too much in the past.

"Professor, we need a cram course in the Great Mahele, when King Kamehameha III's advisors divided up the lands and imposed a western style system on Hawai'ians. We've read some of course, but we need your expertise."

Jon Miller was one of the best known, and most respected, scholars of 19th century Hawai'i in general, and land use in particular.

He was the author of several books and many articles on the details and nuances of the great division.

Miller was glad to help, and to always teach. He began with the overall history of the Great Mahele, how the lands were divided first between the King and the Chiefs, then between the King and the government, and finally how even commoners got a small piece of the 'aina' – the land - to call their own.

"So the first major division had the King with about 60% and the Chiefs with about 40%?" Asked Zoe taking careful notes.

"Right. But this did not give the land directly to the chiefs. They still had to apply to the Land Commission to get actual title. Then the King took his lands and subdivided them between his private lands – or Crown Lands – and government or public lands. But commoners still were left out. So in 1850 they enacted the Kuleana Act where commoners who were already tenants could apply for the land they farmed. And they could then ask for any Crown, government or Konohiki - or chief lands."

"Sounds very democratic, very forward looking," said Kirk.

"Well, yes, in theory. But to get a fee-simple title to the lands people had to first pay to get them surveyed. They also had to legally file a claim with the Land Commission, and then prove that they were cultivating it themselves, and produce at least two witnesses. It was very legalistic, very foreign, and very new on all levels for Hawai'ian commoners. On top of that, there were strict and tight deadlines. In other words, what looked like a fair system to a foreigner, turned out to be pretty daunting to a Hawai'ian."

"But they did get access to the lands, right?"

"In the end, only about one percent of the lands were successfully claimed by the 'maka'aninana' – or commoners. To add insult to injury, the government kept giving the Konohiki, or chiefs, extensions of the deadline, all the way up into the mid-1890s. I'm afraid it never really works out for the common folks. Does that answer all your questions?"

"Kirk, show him the papers," urged Zoe. Daniels pulled from his briefcase several photocopies of original documents. He had not wanted to jeopardize or lose the originals. "We have, shall we say, come across these. Wondering if you could tell us about them."

"OK. This first one is a quote from David Malo, a well-known Native Hawai'ian historian at the time who also was a confidant of the King and his Privy Council. Many believe it was Malo who convinced the King to divide up the lands in the first place. This second one, obviously a page out of the original Land Commission final report in 1855, that is very self-congratulatory about how they were helping the maka'ainana farmers. Nothing new or unknown here."

"What about this one?"

Miller looked intently at the photocopy of the document written in Hawai'ian. He took his time reading it, as he was fluent in the language. A wry smile came over his face. He sighed, and sat down, just nodding to himself.

"I'm not going to ask you where you got this, or the original if you have it. But it is a great example of one of the first actual fee-simple land title awards given to one of those lucky and persistent Hawai'ians who successfully navigated the haole legal system. It is complete, and has the original Royal stamp on it. It gives the name of the original owner of the land, and the metes and bounds of it. Looks like a fairly small piece of land for a farm. But considering where it is, that might not be that important."

"So where is it?" asked Zoe.

"Well I can't be absolutely sure until I do the cross check with modern tax key maps, but I recognize the konohiki section of old Honolulu, the ahupuaa – or mountain to the sea pie-shaped land management unit, the moku, or subdivision. Yep, I'll guess this is a parcel just Makai, ocean side, of Kawaiahao Church, in what came later to be known as Kaka'ako. Of course, over time, people lost their deeds, and in our modern system sometimes land was taken over if taxers were not paid. Often others laid claim and gained title to the land without the original families even knowing about it."

"Let me give you a good but unlikely contact to track this down. If you spend some time in the Kaka'ako area at all, you may well notice an older woman who might well be taken for homeless. Her clothes are often raggy. She actually is a longtime resident who prides herself in knowing whatever goes on, the people, the activities. Her cover is that she feeds the stray cats. She's got a name for all of them. Don't sell her short. We call her the Cat Lady. Find her. Talk to her. Gain her confidence. She may be of help, who knows."

Zoe and Kirk gave each other a look of mixed awe and glee. They asked Miller if he could create an English translation of the document. He readily agreed and said he'd have it in a few days – complete with tax key map references.

Still a little shaken by what they had learned, they splurged at the higher class Japanese restaurant on King Street near Times Supermarket.

Chapter 8

LIFE OF THE HEAVENS

Tuesday, December 20, 2011

Zoe had been doing her homework. With hints from Professor Miller, she already was looking for the Cat Lady. She decided to do a walk around Kakaʻako. Sandwiched among the light industrial car repair shops are the tenacious remnants of an art community. *There is that neighborhood theater on Queen Street.*

– The Prince. Looks like it is on its last legs, she thought. Used to be a lot of neighborhood theaters – spent many a Saturday afternoon watching cartoons with my cousins.

Kakaʻako was a noisy place, and very industrial. She walked passed a greasy moped rental and repair shop. It was next to a square, windowless building for a printing business used by small shops and younger politicians who could not afford the more expensive full color productions.

There is a pottery store, she noted, a fading symbol of what once was a thriving art community that had been pushed out by the industrial operations. On nearly every corner was a bar frequented by blue collar workers after work and well into the early morning hours. And nearby a graffiti covered coffee and sandwich shop – operating under the name *Life of the Heavens.*

She stopped in for a latte – her third of the day – and struck up a conversation with a young Hawai'ian guy operating the expresso machine – Kekoa Potter. She asked about the name of the shop: 'The Life of the Heavens.'

"I'm just the nephew of the owner, helping out occasionally. There has been a shop or a store at this site for over 90 years. My cousin operates the pottery and arts and crafts store," he explained. "My grandfather once made pottery for the Moana Hotel," he bragged. She thanked him and went on, looking for that special someone Professor Miller had told them about.

No one really knew the Cat Lady's full name, but some called her Sally. Zoe met her feeding her feral brood on Queen Street across from the abandoned brick brewery. She remembered reading that a former governor had invested in refurbishing it as an historic building, but it hadn't happened. *That's the story of Hawai'i, great ideas, great plans, but not much follow through,* she sighed.

Sally was obviously proud and protective of the cats.

"This one I call Rabbi, see how that black mark looks like a Jewish cap? There over there is snake eyes, for obvious reasons. And next to him is my favorite, Cheezy. Feed em once a day. They know when I'm coming. They wait. They are my kids."

"Sally, I need your help. I'm trying to find an old Hawai'ian family that used to live in this area. It probably is impossible after all these years, all these changes, but I want to try. Can you help me?" Zoe further explained that the family originally might have been called Keola'o'kalani. It was the name on a Mahele land deed we found.

"A Mahele deed? You talking King Kamehameha the third Mahele?"

"Yes that's what I'm talking about. Professor Miller has been helping us. He suggested we talk to you."

"Jonny sent you to old Sally, did he? I used to baby sit for his niece!" Sally paused and looked intently at Zoe. "I like your eyes, child. I like your voice. I think you care about people, and you take pride in what you do. So Cat Lady will help you. You see that coffee shop down there? The Life of the Heavens?"

"Yeah, I just got a latte from them."

"But the NAME of the coffee shop? First, you need respect the name. It is an old Hawai'ian family name. One handed down. One given with aloha from a royal. It is actually a translation of a treasured Hawai'ian family that can trace its roots back to a Hawai'ian alii. The name was – she paused for effect - Keolaokalani – Life of the Heavens. Rumor has it that different branches of his family have roots in the area, including a man who was a long time projector guy at the Prince Theater."

Chapter 9

....

CINEMA PARADISIO IN PARADISE

Monday, December 26, 2011

It was the day after Christmas. Kekoa had until the end of the month, but he thought he should close out his Uncle's Peter Kalani's affairs as soon as possible and that included removing his personal items from his apartment. It was just over a month since his passing, November.

Uncle Peter lived in a Section 8 housing apartment, and lived off the rental income from a couple of small parcels in Kalihi, and Kekoa believed he would have wanted the apartment cleared and cleaned up so someone else could use it. Affordable housing was so hard to come by in Honolulu. And with all of the million dollar condominiums being built in the downtown neighborhoods there would have even fewer housing units available for the poor and the working class folks. This was something Kekoa knew and experienced firsthand. In fact it was a lifetime experience so far for him.

Even though Uncle Peter had paid the rent for the month, the building managers who were always grateful to have had a good tenant like uncle, and said Kekoa could take his time to pay off the final rent. He had three weeks more, but Kekoa gave himself a week to sort and cleanup. Although other family members and friends offered to help, he wanted to sort out the personal possessions first. He asked that they help with the cleanup.

Uncle Peter was a friendly man who loved his nieces and nephews, but his inner life and interests were always a bit of mystery to Kekoa and other family members. He had a degree from Honolulu Community College, where he majored in Hawai'ian history. He was a frequent visitor to the Cook Museum. He dabbled in genealogy. He hung out at the State Archives on his days off. Yet, he was somehow content to live a simple and reclusive life, with a low paying job at the theater.

It was now three days since Uncle's burial, and Kekoa thought it was time to start. He was taking the responsibility because under Uncle's simple will he left everything, including those small plots in Kalihi, for Kekoa, with one exception. There was also a few dollars in a savings account, and a very small insurance policy which, in the end, would cover the cost of the funeral and the reception. The family had insisted that he be buried in the ancestral graveyard where all the members of the family had been consecrated for decades, going back to the days of the Kingdom.

And a burial plot in those old cemeteries, with their limited space, is quite expensive, Kekoa learned. Still, it was for his Uncle and he was happy to make his farewell and aloha to life and the family a joyous one. The old man had put a small payment down years ago for the plot next to Auntie so they would be together. *The two of them must be happy now.*

But the one exception was a big one. Peter Kalani had title to a strategically placed parcel of land in Kaka'ako. His last will stipulated that the land would go to the one institution he loved more than any other during his life: The Cook Museum.

Kekoa went through old family photo albums. He found several boxes of photos that were loosely kept there. None had been mounted or put in an appropriate album that seemed to go by a particular decade in his life. Kekoa even found a few pictures of himself with family members around. It was Hawai'ian style that since Uncle and Auntie had no kids - and that one or two of the nieces would be pretty much raised by the couple. In the old days it was said you were "hanai" - Hawai'ian for adopted - to the new parents, and you were formally Hawai'ian for adopted - to the new parents, and you were formally transferred to them and raised in all respects as the son or daughter of the new parents.

In Kekoa's time, he was just sent to Uncle and Auntie's nearly every day after getting off the bus from the Kamehameha Schools campus. From the time he went to school, he was to go to their place once school was over, and check in with them first before going out with friends or classmates. When playtime was over, he was to return back for homework and for dinner before his mother or father would pick him up. Most of the time there was another cousin there, but he was the only one who went there nearly every day and on weekends. So they became a second set of parents for Kekoa. They came to his school's open house nights. When neither of his parents could attend a particular PTA meeting, Uncle and Auntie were happy to go for them. When Kekoa got his report, he showed it to all four of them. Uncle and Auntie got to know every one of his teachers. Under that situation, of course he had to maintain good grades in school.

Uncle Peter was older than his dad, and he had a greater familiarity with old Hawai'i. He knew all of the great athletes of the golden years. He knew the baseball players, the football stars, even the sumo wrestlers who came from Japan in the old days like Taiho. He was there when Joe DiMaggio hit a home run at the old Honolulu Stadium. In fact he had seen Elvis Presley sing in a benefit concert to open the Arizona Memorial.

But the stories that Uncle had that thrilled Kekoa the most were about when he was a projectionist for the biggest local theater chain. For most of those years he was the projectionist at the old Prince Theater, which now was just a store, and on previous occasions the start up for a restaurant.

The old movie theatre days were the stories that Kekoa loved the most. When it was time for him to go to movies, the neighborhood theaters were gone, as were the stand alone ones that went the way of IBM typewriters. It was all multiplex theatres now. He wondered what it was like when guys went to Saturday morning matinées for a nickel or a dime, when everyone showed for movies in the afternoons. He couldn't imagine when there was a time when the local movie theatre was the center of a town or of a neighborhood.

He couldn't even begin to imagine when everyone waited to see the latest Elvis Presley movie, much less the John Wayne ones. And who was James Stewart? How could anyone see the Sound of Music a dozen times? But it happened, according to Uncle.

"Kekoa," he would say, "the next time it comes on cable be sure to see the movie *Cinema Paradisio*. That movie come real close to what a movie theater was all about." So Kekoa did see the movie, and in fact several times. It never failed to surprise him about movies in the old days. He kind of wished he were there back then.

Next, Kekoa came across a few letters that had been tied together in a neat bundle. He could never remember Uncle writing many letters, so it drew his curiosity. These letters were not personal correspondence, but were formal ones. Two were with letterhead from a law firm. Three letters from Uncle were hand written. He was schooled in an age where children were taught cursive handwriting. There were two letters apparently from Uncle. It looked like the lawyer's letters were in response to whatever it was that Uncle had sent to them.

He sat down and began to read the letters. Three from Uncle and two from the firm - and judging from the post-marked dates were sent a few years ago. This, before he had gotten sick and was hospitalized.

The first surprise was that Uncle actually also owned more than one plot of land in the Kalihi district. There was a small map, and entered in pencil was the notation: 'Sell and divide profits among my three nephews.' *Wow*, thought Kekoa, *I guess that includes me! How cool that Uncle thought of us. Probably will be enough to buy a new used car.*

Kekoa sat down and began reading the other correspondence. It was something about the piece of property in Kaka'ako. He was stunned to learn that the actual land owned by his modest uncle was the very parcel on which his relatives had built the coffee shop!   In a separate envelope was a letter from the Cook Museum director, thanking his Uncle for his commitment to Hawai'ian history, and his intention to will the coffee shop land to the Museum.

In the second letter from the lawyer, he saw that Uncle Peter had scribbled, "Check wall for box." But there were no other directions, words or clues. Just that. Kekoa didn't know what to make of it. He decided to finish going through the papers and pictures, and then call it a day. But that was not all. Neatly typed was a public notice that was to be printed in a widely distributed newspaper. It read as follows:

PUBLIC NOTICE

Pursuant to the Last Will and Testament of Peter K. Kalani, the following public announcement shall be published in a widely distributed newspaper:

The adoption of Western, non-Hawaiʻian systems of legal ownership of land during the 19th century was not well understood by the people. An alien and cumbersome process was required to make claims, which included the expenditure of funds for measuring boundaries and other fees. Claims had to be made within a certain deadline to be valid. After receiving a Land Commission Award, many subsequently lost ownership due to the inability to pay taxes and the sale of properties that were little understood. A great injustice was perpetrated on the Hawaiʻian people, as ownership was lost to newcomers, including many foreign merchants. I have been the legal owner of land in Kakaʻako, inherited from generations before me, but I recognize that the original claims to such land may have been lost over time. Having no living immediate family, I therefore declare the following:

I, Peter K. Kalani, do declare and so order that following my death, the fee simple ownership of my Ili Ku property (TKM 1620) in the Honolulu Ahupuaa of the Kona Moku of Oahu shall be transferred as a gift to the Cook Museum, provided:

That such transfer shall be delayed for six months following the date of my death; and

That should any citizen of Native Hawaiʻian ancestry come forward with a valid documentation of an original Land Use Commission award (Palapala Hooko) dating from the time of the Great Mahele, that person shall be granted fee simple ownership of this property; provided further that should there be more than one such valid Land Use Commission Award presented, the attorney for my estate, or a successor, shall determine an equitable distribution of ownership.

Claims should be presented to my attorney and executor,

James Roberts, esq. Attorney at Law

While he and Sheri had dinner that night, he told her all about the letters, the two deeds and the public notice, and also reminisced about Uncle Peter's memories of old. According to the lawyer, James Roberts, the public notice and it was due to appear in the papers the next day. He calculated that the property would be transferred to the Cook Museum about mid-April of next year. It was unlikely that there would be anyone coming up with an old deed.

Now that Sheri had been living in the neighborhood and actually working at the Kaka'ako Commission, they would dig up the old maps and go walking looking for what might still be left from that time. Kekoa thought, *who knows? Maybe they'll find this wall. And maybe the box was still there, whatever it was or contained.*

****

Chapter 10

....

YES, GODFATHER

Tuesday, December 27, 2011

Leighton Thomas was used to working late. He was divorced, and his work as executive director of the Kaka'ako Commission was his whole life. He was a Georgetown law graduate, as so many from Hawai'i were. A graduate of the prestigious Hawai'i Prep Academy, his former classmates were the power elite in Hawai'i. They all belonged to the Pacific Club, went to parties at the Yacht Club, and entertained each other in their homes along Kahala Ave. His godfather was none other than Robert Shilling.

Not content to demonstrate his diligence and loyalty in his own efforts, Thomas was hard on his staff. He was famous for lecturing about the "grace of hard work" and "the sins of sloth." He often made the whole crew of twelve stay late before Commission meetings. His fairly new secretary, Sheri Ishihara, was no exception. He liked to say they were all part of the team, but in reality, he pretty much ignored the lower ranking staff, often speaking to others as if they were not even in the same room.

It was one of those nights when Leighton and Sheri were wrapping up at the office, and she was photocopying documents just outside his office that she overheard him on the phone.

....

"Yes Robert, I understand. There is no problem getting the rezoning and permits for the Davis parcel, and the three adjoining properties. Whatever Kono did to convince them…I don't want to know. A year from now, you won't even know that there had once been a shabby walk up on that site," he laughed. "And you know how much I appreciate the favor you are doing for me. God bless you."

The Davis…that's my apartment, Sheri thought to herself. She leaned closer to hear more.

"No problem from the owners, what do they call them, the Mai Tais? You made them an offer, right? Again, no problem with the Commissioners. I'll make sure that the technical briefings show that your development is a 'win-win' for everyone. No, I don't think there is anything to worry about with Prof. Miller or his environmental extremist friends. Nobody cares about the old Hawai'ian burials, or anything else. This town belongs to the Shillings and others who can see the future. No problem here. Yes, I know the 'Love of the Land' group filed a brief to intervene. Guess what, seems I just can't find that brief anymore."

***

"Kekoa I'm telling you they are going to tear down my apartment building. I think Joe and Molly have sold out. And that slimeball Leighton is going to cook the books to make sure the developer godfather of his gets his way. Somebody's got to stop this. Somebody's got to stop Leighton from screwing everybody."

"Gee", said Kekoa, "after all these years, telling you that you always could have a home in their walk up, I'm kind of stunned. We've got to do something. I don't know what, but something." Sheri had never seen him so angry. And Kekoa knew that look in Sheri's eyes, when she got her mindset on something and wouldn't let go. He could hear the wheels turning.

"Well, I know you'll think of something. So, you were going to tell me about your Uncle's papers or something?"

"Yeah, I contacted that lawyer. He said we needed to meet. The deadline for anyone coming forward with a deed will be coming up in a few months.

Chapter 11

···

FINDERS KEEPERS

Friday, December 30, 2011

Sheri, remember me, Zoe, from the Bull's soccer team? Been a few years, huh?" Sheri looked up from the local paper spread out on the coffee house table, pleasantly surprised to see an old teammate, who was now getting pretty famous. She was with a young haole guy.

"Wow, Zoe, great to see you again. Zoe this is my boyfriend Kekoa. What brings you to Kakaʻako?" They gave each other a hug, while Kirk and Kekoa shook hands. "I remember you, you came in for coffee one day. I knew I recognized you. Gee you write for the Manoa, I enjoy reading your stuff."

"Awesome. To think I was buying coffee from Sheri's boyfriend. Do you have a minute, we, ah, this is Kirk Daniels who works at the Cook Museum. We think we have something really important to tell the owner of this shop."

"Well, seems like you are probably looking at him, at least for now," said Kekoa. "My uncle used to own it, but he just passed away, and eventually, Kirk, this is going to be donated to your Museum!!"

"That's what we wanted to talk to you about," said Kirk. They all sat down, and waited for Kekoa to bring them mugs of fresh brewed Kona coffee.

"We have found an old deed to this land, from the 1800s," began Zoe. We wondered if it had any relevance to future developments in Kaka'ako." Sheri almost stood up in shock. "Zoe do you know that I work at the Commission these days?"

"This is unbelievable, but wait, you've got to hear this," said Kirk, who then turned to Zoe to continue the tale.

"Kirk saw the notice in the paper, about your uncle's will. We thought, possibly, we may have actually found the deed, and who knows, this land might even belong to you!"

"What? You found an old Mahele deed?" Kekoa glanced at Sheri in disbelief.

"Yes, you see when that bus ran into the wall at the church, do you remember that in the news? Well in the wall was this old box, and in the box a bunch of papers, including an old deed. Since Kirk works at the Museum, the director, Dr. Apo, who regardless of what you may have heard, is a creepy sexual predator, assigned him the job of investigating the papers and doing the research. I don't think he expected it to be very important."

"What do you mean sexual predator?" Interrupted Shari.

"Never mind, just that he hit on me a few times. Back to the story."

"We took it to Professor Miller up at UH and he translated it," said Kirk. "Found the tax key map, and we think it might be right here."

"So can we see it? Do you have it with you?"

"No. We didn't want to risk carrying it around. Kirk put it in a place where it would not be easily found...or stolen."

"Who would want to steal it?" asked Sheri.

"Well, the Museum for one. But more than that. We suspect the Museum might have a, let's say, understanding with a big developer..."

"Shilling?" asked Sheri.

"That's the one. He is one greedy guy who wants to build huge condos all over the place, including here on this very land. He will kick out all the small businesses and residents, and Kaka'ako will only be for the rich."

"That's not right, that's not 'pono' ",said Kekoa with obvious anger in his voice. Sheri nodded in agreement. "I'd do anything to stop this guy. Sheri you were worried about this. It's more than a coffee shop at stake, I guess."

"That's right," Kekoa, said Zoe with encouragement. "But we think we might have a way to stop all this."

"How?" asked Kekoa, suspiciously. Over the next hour, Kirk explained his scheme to lure Shilling into a scandal, using the deed as bait. Zoe, departing from her role as a reporter, nodded assurances that it would work.

"But Zoe, you are a reporter. Should you be involved in this kind of thing?" asked Sheri warily.

"You are right, Sheri, I usually report just, well, news. But you know, sometimes it gets really, really frustrating, just writing articles that don't actually change anything. Don't get me wrong, I love this job, and I think *The Manoa*, and I personally, do make a difference. But, well, Kirk has a pretty good plan. And I told him, if he can convince you guys to go along, just to try it, well, in the end, you get your land and we get Shilling."

"So when can we get the deed?" asked Kekoa, with a little obvious irritation. "I mean, I don't understand why you didn't bring it?"

"Look," explained Kirk. "If it is what I think it is, maybe I'm paranoid, but I just want to protect it. This could be the key to a whole change in how Honolulu deals with Kaka'ako. The very shape of the city. The way Hawai'ian bones, the sacred 'iwi,' are treated. I mean, this is really big. And that means that the fewer people who know where it is – well I haven't even told Zoe."

"Yeah, it's really big for you, but bigger for me," snapped Kekoa. "Well, sorry, I guess I should be thanking you guys, but just don't forget this deed belongs to me, and I don't want to get lost in all this politics."

"Don't worry. I'll get you the deed. Just as soon as we meet with Shilling," said Kirk.

Later, Sheri assured Kekoa they could trust Zoe, but Kekoa was skeptical. "Maybe it will work, maybe not. I'm not too happy about not getting the deed right away. We'll see."

Chapter 12

THE IZAKAWA

Monday Januar y 2, 2012

Kirk Daniels coasted his ten-speed to a stop in front of Toronaga's. He had never been here before, but he'd heard so much about it...very historical, yet a bit pricy for his taste and salary at the Cook Museum. True to his calling, he did a bit of research on the Japanese roots of Izakaya. He had looked it up on Wikipedia ––although he would never admit to anyone that he used the site.

> An izakaya (居酒屋) is a type of Japanese bar that serves food to accompany the drinks. They are casual places for after-work drinking. "Izakaya" is a compound word consisting of "i" (to stay) and "sakeya" (sake shop), indicating that izakaya originated from sake shops that allowed customers to sit on the premises to drink.

Daniels had tried to copy the kanji (Chinese characters) but his initial attempts were clumsy and didn't look anything like the printed version.

He separated the Japanese decorated 'noron' cloth curtains in the doorway, and entered a different world. It was all wood, it was foreign, and it was engaging. He heard it was run by a quirky guy called Moto.

Moto was one of the first to open an Izakaya in Honolulu.

Moto made okonomiyaki – Osaka style - one of his specialties at his Izakaya

– Toronaga's. To educate his customers, there was a prominent framed definition on the wall:

> Okonomiyaki - a savory Japanese cabbage pancake, Cooked at your table on a flat grill, with choice of various seafood such as shrimp, or pork, veggies, flavorings, and a special Japanese mayonnaise over the top. There are many regional versions, but in Osaka, you can also find okonomiyaki Cookd with octopus, squid, shrimp, sliced chicken, just veggies, scallions, or kimchee.

To add authenticity and ambiance, Moto dressed his waiters and other staff in clothes from the period of 1600 – in honor of Tokugawa (徳川 家康) Ieyasu founder and first shogun of the Tokugawa shogunate of Japan, which ruled after the Battle of Sekigahara in 1600. The interior design was of a typical shop in the early Edo period.

For fun, Moto would often wait on tables himself, but when he did, he donned an imitation Japanese warrior's armor, including an elaborate lacquer helmet to simulate Ieyasu. He became Ieyasu. Local diners loved it. Japanese tourists were directed to it.

Everyone hoped that for their meal, on their night, they would be favored with the service of Ieyasu himself. Other times, in homage to Cavell's novel Shogun, Moto had one of his young staff dress as the foreign pilot – Anjinsan.

But in spite of the attractive visuals, Kirk was focused on finding someone he was to meet – Robert J. Shilling, one of the most successful urban developers in Hawai'i. It was Shilling's idea to come to Toronaga's, one of his regular haunts. A kind of home turf. Normally Shilling would not have given a kid like Daniels the time of day, but the strange phone call had piqued his interest.

"Shilling here."

"Mr. Shilling, my name is Kirk Daniels. I work at the Cook Museum."

"How did you get this number?"

"Never mind that. Trust me, you are going to want to hear what I have to say."

"So say it."

"What if I told you that I have the legal power to derail your planned luxury condo in Kaka'ako?"

"Whattya talkin about?"

"I mean that I can stop your condo if I want to."

"What are you one of these environmental nuts?"

"I think you are going to want to see my evidence."

"Are you asking for a meeting?"

"I think that would be a good idea. I think you are wise to meet."

"OK, I'll meet you if you want."

"At your office?"

"Hmmm. Meet me next Monday, 7:30, at Toronaga's. You know where it is?"

"Is that the Izakaya near Cook Street?"

"Yup. Don't be late."

"I won't."

Shilling hung up. He immediately pulled out his special, private cell phone. Only a small number of confidents had this number, and it was used sparingly.

"Kono here. What's up boss?"

"Need you to check out somebody. Keep it discrete. Find out where he lives, what he does. How he travels, his habits. Name is Kirk Daniels. Sounds young. Sez he works at the Cook Museum.

"No problem."

"Oh not so good news. Need the info by Monday noon."

"Do my best."

"Good. Call me with updates."

When Kirk Daniels walked tentatively into Toronaga's, Shilling already knew a great deal, not only from what Kono dug up, but what his IT specialist could find on the web. He knew Daniels was 27, graduated from a Michigan high school, and U.C. Irving for college. He was 5'9" tall, 150 lbs, didn't own a car and biked everywhere. His girlfriend was a young reporter. He used to work at the Mission Houses Museum, located next to the iconic Kawaiahao Church. Shilling almost didn't show, but what the hell, he was going to eat at Tornonaga's anyway. He sat waiting for Daniels with Kono, a 300 lb. part Hawaiʻian, who, as they say, knew his way around.

Daniels recognized Shilling from his frequent pictures in the paper – one of the aspiring movers and shakers in Hawaiʻi. He saw Shilling motion to his table, located in one of faux wooden tatami booths in the far corner of the restaurant.

"Sit down kid."

"Who's he?"

"My driver. I like to treat my staff right."

"I was expecting just you. What I have to say is…private."

"You want to talk, you talk now, with both of us. You're the one who asked for this."

"OK." Daniels did not speak at first. He was taking in the unique decorations, the staff dressed in Edo era garb, the smells of the sizzling of the okonomiyaki, the smell of beer.

"Want to order something?"

"Well…"

"Kono waved to the waiter. To his surprise, a short man in full Tokugawa armor, including a face mask, sauntered up to the table and bowed.

"Usual order, with pork. Three draft Saporos."

"I hadn't planned to eat but…"

"Forget it kid. If you're going to do business, you've got to do it right. So you work at the Museum?"

"Yeah. I do research. I read a lot of documents. Look at a lot of artifacts. Specialize in 19th century history. Specially look at the time of the Great Mahele, when all the land was divided up, all kinds of people got Mahele deeds. You'd be surprised." Shilling pretended he was all ears, and interested.

Ieyasu came back with the flat grill, and a bowl of creamy batter, which he ladled out into a large lumpy pancake that instantly began to sizzle. Another waiter came over with three frosty mugs of beer, and a few small dishes laden heaping with chicken and other delights – what locals called "heavy pupus," and other dishes of soybeans, boiled peanuts, and kimchee.

All three stared at the cooking food, took a few sips, picked up their chopsticks and pretended to be interested in the side dishes.

"Alright, maybe you can tell me why we are here."

"Do you remember when that city bus ran into the old wall at Kawaiahao Church?"

"I remember. What of it?"

"They found something in that wall. Something that relates to who might own a key parcel of land."

"What land?"

"Maybe it's your land. Maybe its land you need to do big development."

"Maybe? It is or it isn't."

"Let's say it is. Let's say it might even be a deed, a very old deed."

"Ok I'll play your game. Let's pretend it is a deed. Let's pretend it is a deed I might be interested in. Now what?"

"Have you seen this notice in the paper, dated just last month?" Kirk handed him a folded, and partly wrinkled section of the Star Advertiser. Shilling looked at it casually, not remembering seeing it. The notice referred to a specific piece of property that he knew would be ultimately owned by his pal, Dayton Apo...who just might be willing to sell it off to a well-financed developer.

"I might know that there actually is such a deed, and where that deed might be."

"Maybe. Might. Are you going to beat around the bush all night?"

Daniels was imagining that he was dealing as an equal with a very powerful man. This was something new. Something he liked the feeling of. Toying with his prey. He started eating some of the Osaka style pork pancake. Shilling and Kono joined in the eating. The table fell silent. Unknown to them, from his small window in the backroom, Ieyasu – Moto – watched carefully, recognizing that an influential fifty year old businessman would not normally be meeting with a young millennial.

"I do know where this deed is, and believe me, it is not just sitting out in the open. It is where only I know. I am thinking you would very much want to get your hands on this deed. I'm thinking it would be worth a great deal of money to you. Millions actually."

"I am thinking that perhaps, if a certain amount of money went in a certain direction, well, this might get me a look at that deed. Am I thinking right?"

"You are getting warm."

"OK. I am imagining a figure of one million dollars."

"I would say warmer, but not anywhere near hot."

"Would five million be hot, hypothetically, I mean."

"No."

"Ten?"

"Twenty would be hot."

"Who the fuck you think you are? Are you trying to blackmail me?"

"I would never use that word. I'm only sayin…"

"Let me guess, you want the money and a jet ride to Paris."

"I would never take a penny for anything that could be a cultural treasure. You just don't know me."

"What are we talkin about?"

"I made this list of what I would do if I ever was rich. Just a kind of financial bucket list."

"What the hell is a bucket list?" asked Kono.

Shilling ignored him, as Daniels pushed an envelope across the table, and took another bite from the okonomiyaki, and a healthy swig of beer. Shilling pointed at Kono, who ripped it open, and showed his boss a list that included the Mission Houses Museum, the Sierra Club, and a special scholarship fund for native Hawai'ian kids – each with a number written after it. And a special amount deposited into the personal account of one Kekoa Kalani. Daniels was not listed.

"Such a list is a dangerous piece of paper. It could get people into trouble. If such a list were to be…honored…we would need to agree to a process. I would need to see this mythical, hypothetical historical paper you might or maybe know about. I would need to secure possession of it. I would need to know that this list would eventually disappear. You understand what I'm sayin?"

"I understand. I am willing to consider any procedures that might be proposed. I don't want any trouble. I just want to ensure that the profits taken out of Kaka'ako get to benefit the people of Hawai'i. Mr. Shilling, you may think I'm a nut, but I can assure you that I am dedicated to fairness and equitable distribution of new wealth. I'm not in it for myself. I just want it to be right, to be pono."

"Tell you what kid, I'll think about this hypothetical conversation which, come to think of it, the beer, I really can't remember a thing you said. But if Kono here remembers, maybe we will contact you. Got a cell phone number or something?"

Daniels eagerly pulled out a slightly wrinkled business card with his cell and email. Kono took it, and the letter with the list. Daniels just noticed that Shilling had touched nothing. *Smart guy*, he thought.

After Daniels left, Ieyasu showed up again with some very heavy pupus, including shrimp tempura, which he knew was Shilling's favorite, and tako (octopus) poke (seasoned raw fish), which Kono favored. They ate in silence for a while.

"Kono, it would be better if you handled this. I don't want any loose ends, anything that might link me directly with the kid, understand?"

"Don't worry boss. I know how to be discrete. I'll find out about this deed, and clean it all up."

"One more thing. Make sure we set aside that small parcel for my godson's new church."

***

Daniels was feeling heady about the meeting. He thought it went well. He phoned Zoe.

"So how did it go?"

"Just like we planned. They bit. I'm sure we have a deal. They just have to figure out how to get the deed and consummate the deal with no tracks or bread crumbs that could lead back to anybody."

"Oh Kirk, I don't feel good about this. What if they try to do something to you? Do you think they are dangerous? This is some hare-brained scheme, trying to suck them into thinking you are stupid enough to blackmail them."

"Naw. They are just greedy developers. As long as they can make their millions, they will be happy. They think I'm just skimming a little off their net profits, and they will never miss it. What they don't realize is that it's all a bluff to trap them into taking a kind of bribe. Once the real story leaks out they will be finished as developers in this town. And then, when the Mahele Deed gives the land to Kekoa Kalani, we kill two birds with one stone. Kekoa gets justice and we derail a bad development!!"

"Hope you are right. At least we know that the deed is for real if they take the bait. See you at your place later?"

"Yes. We can celebrate."

Chapter 13

....

CHANG'S DELOREAN -AND- WHY PREVENTION IS BETTER THAN THE CURE

Wednesday February 1, 2012

Moto could easily hear the supercharged engine of Chang's DeLorean as it pulled into one of the treasured parking stalls of the Izakaya. It was 3 o' clock, and the restaurant was closed until dinnertime. During the break between lunch and dinner prep the place was quiet. It was a time that Moto enjoyed most. No interruptions. Peace. It seemed like the blissful silence would be shattered forever. Curses on you Chang and all of your ancestors for notinstilling in you the proper Asian values, thought Moto.

"Yo! Moto-san!" Chang bellowed, as he burst through the doors of the Izakaya.

"Charlie, over here," Moto called from the table just to the left of the entrance to the kitchen. This was his favorite table. Everyone knew that. Unless the restaurant was packed, the regulars knew that it was the one table they should never ask for. That is unless, of course, Moto was already sitting there. It became part of the practice of the regulars to first check, very nonchalantly, if he in fact was sitting there. If it was empty they would then tell the maître de their other preference. If they were lucky and he was already sitting there, then the regulars would ask if they could join Moto at his table. But not until then, and under those very circumstances.

If you were lucky, and he was there, and if the supervising headwaiter knew you as a regular, you were blessed with the escort over to join Moto. There, Moto would help you order. He knew in advance what was particularly good that particular day. This is because he did all of the shopping for fresh food items that very morning. All the merchants knew that they were to expect him, and they all saved their very best catch or find of the day, or their best produce if it was a farmer's market. Moto always paid top dollar, and never forgot the kindness of the vendors. Throughout the year they could expect regular meals sent over from the Izakaya for family and workers. And Moto always prepared those meals just as if they were regular diners at the restaurant.

Moto also understood better than any sommelier the pairing of wine or something from Quincy Adams, or Aso Extra Dry beer, or Morning Dew Shochu, with a particular meal. In fact, his treasured skill was his mastery of the pairing of sake to a particular meal. His mind was a treasure trove of knowledge. It had been said many times, that if you were a regular customer he had never forgotten any meal that you had ever ordered in all of your visits to his restaurant. He never hesitated to interject: "No, my friend, I think you would much rather like..." Or, "Most times Moto agree with you, but this particular beverage, which I lucky to find, go even better with that dish. 1998 was very good year."

Of course when Chang came, he would never ask for a particular table. He would simply walk over to Moto's table whether he was sitting in it or not. That, is unless customers were already there. If Moto was already entertaining, Chan would just walk into the kitchen, where he knew all the help, and they all knew what to do. They would set a place for him in Moto's side office. No one else in Hawai'i, much less Japan, or the rest of the world, had that same privilege.

Chang himself had a vast knowledge of wines, beers, and other liquors. He even had a fair knowledge of sake. But on that he always deferred to Moto's selections. Moto himself made the same deference: Chang had an encyclopedic knowledge and sensibility about Chinese cuisine. He understood all the different dishes and specialties of each of the provinces. He could also cook with the best chefs in Hawai'i.

For ten generations many members of his family were chefs. So Moto, who never deferred to anyone when it came to food ingredients, preparation and taste, would defer to Chang on Chinese cuisine. They would never argue over food and beverages, except in one area. Chang also loved fast foods. Moto hated them. The only time he was ever seen at a fast food establishment would be when Chang said they had to meet right away, and he was hungry, and didn't have but a half hour. And so they met where Chang selected. Moto never ordered anything, except for fries… "No salt, please." And please to give me extra catsup." Moto's practice was to drown the fries in catsup. This was the only way he could handle it.

To all that Chang would always throw in: "Moto-san, you gotta try with the bacon and cheese and at the same time would open up his burger. You want half? Happy to share with my buddy, you know. You always treat me at your place but you never let me pick up the tab here 'cepting for the fries. And you only order small. Get the super duper super fries! They mo' ono, you know, Moto!"

Chang went straight to Moto's table, since that was where he sat between the two dinner preps and service. "There you are!"

"Charlie, Moto hear you coming from a block or two away. Why don't you get a quiet car? You can just put the alarm signal on when you're in pursuit. All your fellow officers do that when they use their car instead of the official police cars."

"Moto-san, I always tell people this car is Moi! Everybody laughed at me when I bought it years ago. They said the company is bankrupt. They made jokes. Eh! Who's laughing now? Do you know how much the last DeLorean went for at the No. 1 car auction in America? Six figures! High six figures. And it was nowhere as good as mine. Eh! Imagine, a car owned by the famous Honolulu Chang! The price would double. Who knows triple!"

"And I don't care if people can hear me across town. I am not touching the original parts. I'll get around to fixing it, when and if I find the right parts."

"That problem. You no fix. Moto know something about cars - you change the muffler so is even louder than should be. You like car sound half way across town. I think you just below the legal limit."

"That's what you don't understand, Moto-san. You so Japanese and so proper. I want them to hear me coming. I keep telling you that. Prevention is the best medicine. Applying or trying to find a cure after the disease has broken out is too late. People get hurt. They get sick; they die."

"Yes prevention. You right. Prevention best medicine. If police officers could prevent the crime before it even start, there will be less pain, less people hurt. On that we agree."

"Okay! I tell you what: now you have chance to be the DeLorean."

"Moto tell you story. Six months ago, big zoning hearing at Kaka'ako Commission. You know they call it KC. Moto curious, so went to the last major hearing. For sure, Moto concerned about the development and how much development. Real estate people tell me especially when the rich guys come to eat at my place: Hey Moto! You going be rich restaurant owner. Think of the millionaires and billionaires who going come over. You can double, no triple maybe, even quadruple price and they'll still going come. No matter how much you charge, you still going be cheaper than New York City and San Fran or LA. Beaucoup bucks Moto-san. Eh! No forget me now?" "Crazy people. Moto like serving local folks. They enjoy my food, and that most important thing. I already own place and the building improvements all paid for. How much money you need? You want friends and family, that enough. I raise prices and that's it. The old gang, their friends and family going someplace else."

"This was six months ago. Why are you telling me now?" Asked Chang.

"Be patient, Chang san. So Moto go to hearing. Plenty people there, I tell you. Big shot developers, especially Mr. Shilling. Of course he there. He's the biggest frog in this pond called Kaka'ako. His man Kono, of course there and on his right hand side. I see the press including the cutsy kid from the UH with that new paper, the *Manoa Investigator*. And plenny environment gang and intellectuals, the Chambus businessmen, big store owners, small store owners who want to cash in. Of course had plenny small storeowners who going lose out.

"All depend which side of the steam roller you on. But Chang-san, I see some other people. They make for more interesting possibilities."

"Like who else there? Seems the way you talk everybody in town there but humble Charlie Chang!"

"Well, first you had the Mai Tais. They not only there, they tesify for the re-zoning. Eh? How you figger that one?"

"So who else?"

"Ah! Now you interested. There your friend and comrade in arms, Stan Takahashi. He not looking official or showing off his badge like he does, so Moto guess he there because he one concerned citizen."

"Concerned citizen---my okole. Stan only concerned about one thing---himself."

"Precisely, as you like say. So I thinking. But Chang, what going get you even more is who he was sitting with."

Now visibly perking up, Chang demands "Who?"

"Well if Mr. Kono some right hand man – I know this Kono, mean person; Takahashi when he off-duty and at hearing sit on Shilling left side. So he left hand man. And that guy in the center he's the guy in the center of Kaka'ako ---Mr. Robert J. Shilling himself. Kaka'ako's savior."

"Interesting. A lot to chew on and understand, just by who showed up."

"Wait, there more. One more person catch Moto attention, a Mr. Kirk Daniels."

"Who?"

"Bright eye, bushy tail, as you Americans like to say. Working on doctorate in archaeology, and one more in anthropology at

University. He testify they need slow down. Get much important information they need to have. When he say that, Shilling no seem to be too happy. Not mad, but not happy too."

"I wonder why this kid is getting mixed up in this."

"Well Charlie-san, Moto give you another story that going catch your attention." Moto then proceeded to tell Chang about the dinner at his restaurant when Shilling and Kono were about to place an order. He told Chang about Kirk coming to the Izakaya and confronting Shilling.

"Shilling was sitting with his man, Kono. Moto think that Mr. Kirk so intense and so full of energy and righteousness that he not even see Kono, only Mr. Shilling, and chance to be hero, and save environment, and save Hawai'ian culture and people."

"Moto, where is this going?" With a flourish, Moto slapped a newspaper in front of Chang. Chang took his time to read the public notice.

"I see why you're concerned. You suspect Kirk thinks he'll stop a billion dollar development by waving a piece of paper. He would be more lucky waving a red flag in front of a raging bull. What is it about these tree huggers, anyway!"

"At first, Moto no understand. No more trees in Kaka'ako. Cut down long time ago. Maybe he hug historic Kaka'ako Theatre. What else get for save here?"

Chapter 14

··

A NIGHT AT THE MUSEUM

Monday, February 6, 2012

It was part of the standard operating routine at the station that each detective had to be available one night of the week, unless he or she was on vacation, to be the detective on call if any incident should occur requiring an investigative officer. Charlie always took Tuesday nights and it was his by seniority, anyhow. He had always preferred Tuesday, because it was the worst night for television shows. Chang could never get into the routine of using the new high tech equipment and so he depended on the standard schedules. Chang remembered growing up, how he would be behind what the rest of the country was watching. His cousins on the mainland would always tease him how backward he was, and how he might as well have been living in Asia or even Africa.

Tuesday nights was also the best time for dinner reservations, not that Charlie made any. He always considered fine dining to be meals at a great Chinese restaurant where he knew the number one chef. He always got the main chef. He knew them all and he was always welcome in the kitchen. In fact, he would never make an order until he had been to the kitchen, and knew what the best ingredients that were available for that particular night. This was his standard procedure when the wife was still alive, and when he had his children living at home. Now that he was living alone, he saw no reason to change his ways. The chefs all noted that he had become even more particular these days. He only had to choose for himself, and not take into consideration what the wife and the kids would want. Back then, he felt that he had to accommodate their slightly more proletarian, no, pedestrian tastes.

It so happened that the break-in at the world famous Cook Museum had occurred and been reported late that evening. Since the report came in late, Chang had already been to dinner. He was just lying in the living room going over the dinner items that he had ordered. The chef at the restaurant had wanted, just like buddy Moto, a precise recap of his views and critique. Nothing less would do, and the special service would require such. It never mattered to Chang since he was happy to serve.

That night he had gone to Ching's Shanghai Buffet. Ching's was an all you can eat buffet. It was also in a neighborhood of working class folks with big families. They were the best customers, and they often could not distinguish between the dishes and the quality of the cooking and the ingredients. You give 'em a lot, and they were happy as can be.

But Chang liked Ching's for two reasons. One was official business. It was a family buffet and it was cheap. It catered to the working class. Chang found, that on occasions, you could spot a parole or probation violator who just had to take the family out to dinner, or to take baby daughter or son for their birthday party. It couldn't be helped. Of course Chang never caused a scene there. And because he knew what it was like to be a father, he always waited until dinner was over, and they were in the parking lot. He even was gracious there. He just quietly walked to the offender and told him he knew who he was, and that he should take the family home, and then later report to the station. It always worked, and probably could only work here in Hawai'i. The guilty were in happy spirits and appreciated the thoughtfulness. Besides they all knew of Chang's reputation. Escape was useless.

The other reason Chang came on Tuesday nights was a little known pattern at Ching's. Tuesday nights was a night that the cooks could do some experimentation on new dishes. In fact it was so freewheeling, that other cooks came from other restaurants if it was their night off to join in the preparation of new dishes or new styles. Chang was the only person who was not a professional chef who knew of this. Of course Moto did too, since when it came to cuisine Chang always shared his knowledge with Moto. Moto always came late since he had to close out his kitchen first.

Driving to the Museum, Chang kept thinking about the night's entrees. The set of herbs that were used on the moi was real ono. *I had never had anything like that with that particular fish. I don't think it would go well on mahimahi, though. Who knows? I will recommend that he try it. And the chicken should have been pan seared first I think. I'll tell Wing that when I go to his restaurant this weekend. It will be fabulous, I think, when he does it that way. I can't wait to taste it. Well, there's the museum.* Chang could see the lights from the freeway. He turned onto the off ramp.

Good old Kalihi. I always feel at home here.

He parked his trusty DeLorean in the stall nearest to the entrance with enough room to open the wing door. The evidence collectors and their chief were already on the job. They were well trained. Clare Song, chief forensic investigator, always made sure of that. "Hey if Inspector Chang is on the case, you always leave a parking space for him. Don't let him waste his time looking for parking. And always leave the space closest to the entrance open for him. You gotta show respect. He's never failed to solve a case yet."

In making that last remark, forensic investigator Clare Song did stretch the truth a little, but just a little. There was this one, but she was the only one who knew about it.

Chang entered the main building. The assistants' workrooms were all off to the backside. Chang took his time. He always loved going to the Cook Museum, even when he was just five years old. That giant skeleton of the humpback whale never failed to bring a whistle to his lips. He whistled now. Love that whale. He would fade back into Moby Dick:

Just call me Ishmael. Some years ago---never mind how long precisely---having little or no money in my purse and nothing particular to interest me on shore, I thought I would sail about a little and see the watery part of the world.

Chang knew the entire opening by heart, and he knew it from the time he was only nine years old. *Hmmm, never mind how long precisely....Ish sounds a little like Moto san.* While he was pondering that connection he heard a voice yell out.

"Inspector Chang! You're here. We're just starting to wrap up things. I can give you a run down now, and the rest will be in my written report, which as you know, you can expect by 10 tomorrow morning."

"Clare you never disappoint but come here. Stand under this magnificent whale with me." She came over and looked up.

"I never get tired of seeing this and standing under it. The Kingdom of Hawai'i was a wild place at that time. Fortunes could be made if one was strong enough. Did you know Lahaina, not New Bedford or Nantucket, or any place on the East Coast was the whaling capitol of the world? Some five hundred whalers were homeported there."

"And the Kingdom," he continued, "was the trade capitol of the Pacific. Why, the sandalwood trade, if truth be known, ran into the millions annually. And Lahaina grew because it could grow Irish potatoes on its mountain slopes. And our ancestors, note we must speak softly on this, had an opium den on every block. The trade in opium was then legal, of course, and made huge fortunes. They say all the blue blood Chinese in Hawai'i had a den somewhere. Sherlock Holmes, if he had ever left England, would have patronized them. Maybe he would have never left this paradise."

"Is it any wonder some of the greatest writers of the era had to come to Hawai'i. Robert Louis Stevenson, himself said, some of his writing here was as good as any he ever accomplished. Jack London felt he had to make a pilgrimage. Mark Twain got his start here. He dreamed of always coming back to Hawai'i. Melville lived here for a few months and did some writing here. Thoreau didn't think he had to leave Concord but even he felt compelled to make a reference to the Sandwich Isles in his book, Walden, and he had some friends who were on the first American scientific expedition into the Pacific and going to the Hawai'ian Islands. Oh, it goes on and on. But what do you have for me?"

"Well, we don't have any prints, at least for now. I'll make a final judgment on that later. The night watchman said that there was no sign of a break-in, but the door was unlocked. He said that from time to time, workers have been careless. He was tied up on another project and didn't make his rounds until very late in the evening. He only realized there had been a break-in when he saw one of the assistant's cubicles. It had been trashed, and a lot of things smashed."

"So if there was theft or if anything was broken, it would have been something belonging to the assistant?"

"Nothing important missing or broken then?" asked Chang.

She explained that Dr. Apo had briefed her. Assistants are always working on projects involving things that are the Museum's property and so these could be very valuable, in fact priceless. Pre-contact artifacts; property formerly belonging to the royalty; even jewelry would be handled by the assistants. There are specific rules about the care of the items and how they must be returned at the end of every day. But no one follows the return policy because of all the research that must go into identifying, and more importantly cataloguing, the thousands of items that come into the possession of the Museum each year.

"Do you have name of the assistant?" "Yes, a Kirk Daniels."

Chapter 15

HOT BOWLS OF CHILI

Friday, February 9, 2012

Takahashi here" said Officer Stan Takahashi when he answered the office line at the station. "Oh it's you. Wass- up? You want to meet? Well, I get off in a half hour. Say, the usual Zippy's in an hour?" "Got it!"

An hour later Officer Takahashi without his work clothes was sitting down at a table at the very first Zippy's next to the one of the busiest middle schools in Honolulu. Takahashi liked to meet there because in midafternoon, when school had let out, the place was flooded with kids. They made a loud racket and it was easy to carry out important, confidential conversations covered by the noise of meaningless teen-age gibberish.

"Well Kono, haven't had to meet with you in a long while. I was beginning to think you folks have been using another person to carry out your work. Of course, I can't believe anyone would do your boss' work for as cheap as I have been doing it for these past ten years."

It had long been a sore point with Takahashi that Shilling didn't appreciate his work, and didn't value it in terms of a decent monetary standard. Whenever he asked for more, Kono would say: "Hey you know I don't set the rates and if I ask I know what the boss would say, 'go get someone else.'"

This time Kono anticipated the usual reluctance that Takahashi would exhibit in hopes of increasing his payment. And Kono knew that it had been quite a while since the boss had any need for "information." So Kono decided he would cut straight into the news Takahashi had been hoping for. But first the important things.

"So Taka, I asked to meet so the treat's on me."

"Well, if you or the boss really wanted to pick up the tab we would have at least met at Toranaga's. I know that's his favorite spot in town."

"Come on - bull! You know I'm picking up the tab and it has nothing to do with the boss. He thinks we meet at a park or even at the parking lot across the station. It's my loss when we come here. And besides, it's your favorite spot."

"Okay, okay. I'll have the usual big bowl of chili and the special of the day---the pork chop."

"Usual drink?"

"Yeah, large root beer."

At the drive-in side you had to go to the counter to order. As Kono placed the order, he enjoyed making Takahashi stew a little.

Handing the chili and pork chp to Takahashi, Kono said, "Here you go. I went with the roast pork. Now before you begin eating, Taka I got some good news for this next assignment should you take it...."

"Have I ever refused?"

Ignoring that, Kono went on. "Well, you know da boss got a big project for Kaka'ako. Da biggest ever for him, for the neighborhood, for the City, hell for the whole state."

"Everybody knows that. So what."

"Da boss, he don't want nothing to go wrong. Yeah going get the usual protests...."

Interrupting, Takahashi said, "With a project this size---I've been following the news Kono, it's easily near a billion dollars. Maybe two, when it's finished for all I know, and wouldn't be surprised. Every tree hugging haole and wise ass local conservationist and their groups are already talking stink about the project and how it shouldn't be built. In fact, you already had that nasty first hearing with the Commission when they did the rezoning. And the radical Manoa paper keeps writing stories…just egging them on."

"Well, da boss, he not too worried about the KC. And issuing the actual special building permits. The commission guys all know him and trust that he delivers on his promises."

"What promises, Kono?"

"Oh you know the boss. He always promise to deliver the project on time. The unions all with him. He got the guys with the big bucks in line, and he can handle the environmentalists."

"Yeah, well he got burned last time by the Sierra Club guys, especially when they when team up with the Hawai'ian groups and their lawyers."

"Well, that was the exception to the rule. And besides it was his law firm that screwed up. They learned. No shit! Boss got a new law firm and he has backup---some mainland lawyers who check up all the time to make sure the local guys doing it right. So no worry 'bout that kind stuff, it's in the bag."

"But this time the boss met some punk haole kid from the mainland. You know the boss can always smell when something might be different, and maybe going get surprise this time. He not really worry about the kid---and you saw him at the first hearing back last June."

"Oh yeah there was some wise ass---who think he hot shit haole boy who was telling the commissioners what they supposed to do."

"The boss think he can handle and he not that worried. But the boss like I wen say can smell something. And he thinks the kid so unpredictable, you don' know what he going do. And then there is this crazy long shot will for a dead landowner…gives up to six months if anyone produces a valid deed."

"You want me to maybe dig up stuff on him. But hard for do since he one malahini. How long he been here."

"As far as I know not very long. No family connections. He not poor so he no need money. Boss say the usual stuff not going work. So the boss to ask you to check him out. Make your usual surveillance. Eh, who know maybe he one pervert or druggie. Anything the boss can use will be one trump card for him. So wat you tink Taka? Can do?"

"Well, give some background info. Anything you guys already know." Takahashi was trying to think about what he could do to make it more worthwhile for him.

"Well, he from the mainland, Michigan then California we told. The guy working on his doctorate. Supposed to be one smart boy. He doing work on old kind stuff."

"Archaeology."

"Yeah, I always get hard time for say a word. He going be one archaeologist. He already get job in archaeology. This guy Kirk Daniels stay work at the Cook Museum. He in department headed by Dr. Dayton Apo. I thought he was related through my auntie's husband side, the one that when marry the guy from Kauai, but he not."

"Hmmmm. Yeah, I think I can be a big help to the boss." *What luck*, Takahashi thought. He had already been to the Cook Museum. He knew Dayton Apo going back to small kid time.

"Okay so I tell the boss, you in. And Taka, boss say when project get through, going get bonus for you."

"Yeah, wat?"

"Well, boss say that all depend. Guarantee going get some bonus but the more you wen help the mo beeg the bonus going be. So the mo' hard you work, the mo' beeg da bonus. All up to you."

"Okay, now time for eat. You know, I tink yo can eat Zippy's chili three times a day and one mo' bowl befo you go sleep."

****

Chapter 16

TWO MAI TAIS COMING UP!

Wednesday, Febr uar y 14, 2012

The Mai Tais' apartment also served as the office for their business of running the small apartment building. They made enough from the rent to pay off the mortgage, to buy the 12- unit place ten years ago. They could maintain the place, but they were slow to fix things due to the cost. They ate well and had weekend entertainment so long as the movie ticket prices didn't go too fast. They could take a two-week vacation a year. They owned a ten-year old Toyota.

But for Joe and Mollie it wasn't enough. They didn't anticipate the high cost of living in paradise. Sure, they had expectations of a good time, but they were willing to live less than royalty.

So, on a weekly basis they would talk about selling the place and moving to Florida or Arizona, or the mecca for the local folks in Hawai'i ---Vegas, baby! And for their annual vacation, Vegas was the place of choice. For each of the ten years, they lived here, they did go to Vegas. The charter flights were so cheap, and they would stay at the California Motel and not have to spend too much for their rooms. Still they were not satisfied.

But whenever they felt like they should pull up stakes and go to one of those happier hunting grounds, they would walk across to Ala Moana Beach park with their handy and portable on-wheels cooler and two chairs, go to their favorite spot. They became such a fixture that locals had become so accustomed to seeing them there. They would sit under the big banyan tree, pour themselves a bunch of mai tais, and enjoy the view, the ocean, the mountains above Punchbowl. The best days were when the big ocean cruisers would pull out. Mollie would say, "Next year, I tell you Joe, we're going to be on it."

Though she had said that to Joe for several years, now, this time, it looked like it was going to happen. When Kono knocked on their door last year, he introduced himself as an aide to Mr. Robert August Shilling. "You might have heard of him, the big time developer."

"Oh yes! Everybody in this town has heard of Shilling. Never actually met the man. Wouldn't mind though."

"Well, Mr. Shilling would like to meet you."

"Joe was shocked. Mr. Shilling....meet with me? Now WHY would he want to?"

"I never get involved in the boss' business. I just do as I am told. We will contact you soon."

Then that opportunity came knocking a few months ago---Kono, Shilling's chauffeur, right hand man and whatever else he might have to do or had done for him. Some say he was Green Beret, or a member of the Special Ops team, or even a member of the elite Navy Seals. But several months ago he came, and very courteously knocked on their office apartment.

"Mr. Shilling has asked me to come to your office and ask if you would like to join him for dinner. He almost always has his business dinners at Toranagas. If you are able to attend, I will take you over to see him. I will wait while you dress. I'm parked in the one guest parking that you have." Kono politely nodded and left.

The Mai Tais were awe-struck. But they knew what to do. They hurriedly dressed and dashed out to the waiting limo.

It became a night that the Mai Tais will remember forever, they vowed. The purpose for meeting was to hear directly from Shilling an offer to buy their property. Shilling's offer was over a half million dollars more than Joe had even dreamed he could get. But Joe didn't want Shilling to think he was pushover, just cause Shilling was rich. So Joe asked for a million more.

"Joe, I can call you Joe? I've had the property appraised by three of the best in town. I never make an offer unless I know for certain what the property would sell for on the open market, give or take a few thousand. I then give the top dollar. You, my friend, need to get your feet on the ground."

"Well I'm sorry my good man, but take it or leave it. I, too, understand value and that's what the property is worth."

Even though they would not actually shake hands that night, the deal was as good as made. And so it was. The sale was contingent on the Commission giving final approval for the project. But Shilling felt confident. And back then, Joe and Mollie also felt good about how things were turning out for them. Finally paradise was going to be affordable. And more than that, they could live with class. They were going to be somebodies.

It was February 14, Valentine's Day, which for some reason, Molly always confused with the Japanese celebration of Boys Day - May 5th, Five Five. Since Molly loved to dabble with what she considered "local," she had just finished hanging out the long silky carp from the tiny back lanai. This only puzzled their 70 year old tenant, Mr. Yanagi. *Dez haoles are one beeg mistry*, he thought to himself.

The phone rang and Joe answered. "Oh Mr. Shilling, it's you. No you don't have to thank me for appearing before the Commission last year. After all, you guys wrote the testimony, so it was a piece of cake. I was happy to do it. After all, we both have vested interests in watching your project gain steam, get the approvals, and get built."

"Oh you have another request. Sure whatever I can do! We're in this together."

"You want me and the old lady to keep an eye on that Kirk fellow if he should show up in our neighborhood? I know he came to the hearing, and there will be more days of building permit hearings ahead, but why would he want to come here? He said he works at the Cook Museum, up in Kalihi Valley and he works on his PHD. So I expect he'll be digging at the old Hawai'ian Heywows or whatchacallems. Yeah, yeah, heehaws, whatever. Aren't most of them on the outer islands?

"Do you think he's just going to work on making trouble for you? In that case, we better keep track of him. Well, I know what he looks like. So does Mollie. And we get around a lot here in the neighborhood. I can tell some of my apartment residents to help out. If you got a photo and can email it to me, I'll share it with the rest of my apartment residents. I'll just say that I've seen him snooping around and some of the property owners suspect he might be the burglar who's ripped off a few units this year. Okay Mr. Shilling, we'll keep an eye on the bastard for you. Hope you remember this when it comes time to close the deal."

Joe hung up and then yelled out: "Hey Mollie come over here. I got some news for you. That was Mr. Robert Shilling himself. You're going to be doing a lot of shopping at Marukai and Long's from now on. And when we have mai tais at the park, we need to watch more than sunsets."

"What's that? Well, you need the exercise, Joe. The walking will do you good. Me? Somebody's gotta watch the office."

***

It was Takahashi who had told Henry Doyle, the unfortunate bus driver, about the changes to Kaka'ako. "Deres goin be big changes, Henry. All the old hangouts probably are going to go. The place we play cards, maybe would be OK. When the old leases expire, or the big guys buy their land, kaput. There will be no places left for us blue collar hard workers to enjoy ourselves."

"Can't you do anything about it?" pleaded Henry.

"Henry, I'm a cop. I hav to be careful. I'm just telling you, its not just the developers. The enviornmentalists, the tree huggers, they don't like the industrial repair shops – the ones we hold our card games on the second floor. If we locals don't stop these do gooder haoles, they will take away everything." As he said this Takahashi looked into Henry's eyes, searching to see if the not so subtle hint was registering. Takahshi knew that it was the developers who really threatened their gambling, but his goal was to plant that seed that the problem was more the young mainlander.

"Maybe somebody else has to do something about it," said Henry. "People like me, they take away my job, now they take away my enjoyments. I don't know Taka, I'm just getting fed up, you know? I'm sick and tired of this shit. I wake up every day and I'm already pissed off before breakfast. Maybe somebody should meet him in an alley and teach him one lesson."

"Henry, I'm going to pretend I didn't hear that. But if that happened, well, some people get what they deserve, know what I mean?"

***

He never saw it coming. Kapiolani Boulevard had some uneven sidewalks, so there was no alternative to skirting along the right side of road, careful not to slide into one of the water drains. He was just near the Jack in the Box when out of nowhere a rusty Honda came just close enough to brush his arm and send Kirk and his bike skidding into the sidewalk near the fast food parking lot.

It took Kirk Daniels a few minutes to recover, sitting on the pavement, collecting his thoughts, resigned to the everyday thrills of riding a bike in the city. Shrugging it off, he peddled off down the road.

Detective Stanley Takahashi had been sitting in his parked unmarked SUV across the street. He watched as Daniels had flipped onto the concrete sidewalk...he recognized the car that had swiped Daniels, and smiled to himself.

Chapter 17

···

BEING THERE

Sunday, February 26, 2012

It was just after sunset. Dying rays of sunlight still dimly and briefly lit the skies over paradise. Seniors were still winding their way around the sidewalks of the park. Diamond Head was green, and young mothers were pushing strollers and comparing notes - bragging about Joanne or Johnny with other mothers. Surfers were getting in their last rides of the day. Children were getting their last dip in the Pacific Ocean, while dads and Big Brothers and Big Sisters were yelling at them to come in and take showers because they were just about finished with the grilling, and it was suppertime. "Any you guys hungry?" cries went out.

Several miles away in Palolo Valley, Henry Doyle wasn't hungry. Or at least for a time there was something more important was on his mind. He said to himself: *Well let's get this over with. And then I'm getting some Korean Kalbi and some of that makkoli. Shouldn't have played cards last night till two am. But I was sure my luck was about to change.*

WRONG! He thought again. He almost let out an angry shout to the parking stall. *Oops. Well, maybe tonight. Yes it will be tonight. Be positive, you ass. Luck is going to change and it begins right now. I'm going drive up to the haole boy's apartment and I am going to tell this Kirk he has to give me the deed Detective Take tol me about. Got to make sure he don't sell it to the highest bidder, like they always do. And if he doesn't, I'm going to beat the kukai out of that guy. Haole boy! You just like the other haoles, you think you can steal from the Hawai'ians. These are my people and I no going let you do that.*

Doyle made the left turn off Waialae Ave at the MacDonalds. *Wat the f....dere he is.* He saw Kirk biking up the valley road. He had on his backpack with UH Warriors splashed all over. Kirk wanted to fit in. *Yeah but you neva go UH you liar buggah! Well eat my dust, you haole. I'll just get a Big Mac, then cruise up and wait for you.*

Thirty minutes later, Doyle got out of his car. He double-checked the mailboxes to make sure he got the right apartment unit---3-C. Okay here we go. He found the stairs and started walking up. He reached the third floor. *Well Mr. Kirk now that I beamed up, no thanks to you. I mean why you don't choose one apartment building with one elevator?* But feeling very good today in spite of losing money all of last night, Doyle laughed at the joke he had made to himself.

Yeah Kirk, you don't beam me up, I'll just beam the crapola out of you. He even laughed out loud that time. "Oops, lucky nobody stay", he said.

He found 3-C. Okay, what no doorbell! I mean doorbell not working. *Go fix'em haole boy.* He gave the door a moderate rap followed by several more. No one came. He knocked a few more times, ever more loudly. He put his ear to the door and heard nothing.

Damn you. He almost said it aloud and in anger. *Okay, haole boy not here. His girlfriend not here. I'll just go in and check it out. Maybe I can find the deed by myself.* He put one hand on the doorknob and the other against the door and was going to see how tight the fit was.

No! Henry! You was stupid once when you wen call while you was driving. No make more stupid mistake and break in. So I gotta wait. Hurry up, haole boy. But tonight, I going get you. If you no geeve me, try wait, I going buss you up beeg time!

About an hour later another man showed up at the apartment building but it wasn't Kirk. It was Kekoa Potter, someone Doyle did not recognize.

He walked up the several flights of stairs and was soon at 3-C.

Well, Kirk, hope you're home. We need to talk. I know you got the deed. I need to see it. I'm getting nervous and my lawyer says I should get it, he rehearsed to himself.

Okay, I know you mean well, haole boy but this is big stuff and it's my stuff. My property. I don't know what I'm going to do with the property yet, but main thing it's mine. I going make the decisions. Not some guy from the mainland. Plus I need. I'm just tired of being poor. And Sheri and I can finally get married. I promised her long ago that it's not going to happen so long as I'm poor. I know too much about what it's like being poor and living off all your relatives.

I mean, I'm grateful they all pitched in to help me---Hawai'ian style – but now I need to make it by myself and maybe even later on, pay back to them for all their kokua and aloha.

With that, Kekoa knocked on the door. He knocked again several more times in succession, each time louder. No answer. He leaned against the door with his hands and had his ear again the panel, hoping to hear something like Kirk's voice on the phone or music playing or the TV on or something. Anything to let him know if Kirk was in.

Okay you're not home. I can wait. But tonight is it! Not going to let you play around with my future and what belongs to me. I'm the new Hawai'ian. We're not keeping quiet when someone is playing around with our land. Not any more, haole boy! Hurry up and come on home. Just come and get it!

Unknown to Potter, Doyle waited along the dark and partly forested road in his car, wondering what this other guy was doing. *Did I see him go to the same apartment? Hard to see, but strange he came right down and is sitting in his car. What the hell is going on?*

While all this was going on, Kirk Daniels had stopped to have a beer with a friend halfway up the valley. His friend was not home so he started out for his apartment up the road.

Leighton Thomas pulled his car into the guest park stall at the apartment. *I can't believe it. I'm driving here and who do I see? Kirk on his bike. What is it, a mile away? I'll sit here and wait.*

Damn you Kirk! I had everything worked out for Schilling. If he got his permits, he promised land to build my church – my dream. Then you come and spoil everything. After all my hard work. A little longer and I was going to collect. I was going to do God's work. Now,

And it's was not for me. No I'm not greedy. I can finally leave this job; finally leave kissing up to people. I can finally go on and do God's work. With my reward, I could open my own branch church with the New Saints and Disciples. I would have had the money to buy in. I could have moved back home and be embraced as a success. All my classmates laughed at me. Who's going to laugh now?

I kept the faith with you Lord. You know I did. I've been better than good! AND IT 'S ALL IN YOUR NAME AND FOR THE GREATER GOOD OF US LOST SOULS.

DAMN YOU KIRK. I WISH YOU WERE DEAD. You don't even go to church, I bet. Probably living with a girlfriend. In sin! With you dead, this would be over. YES DAMN YOU KIRK! YOU DESERVE TO DIE! I PRAY TO THE LORD ABOVE TO STRIKE YOU DOWN!

Oh no! What am I saying? Oh forgive me lord. Heed not my words. No! No! No!

Oh Kirk, just hurry and show up. Let me just talk to you. Let me make you understand. You can't win. Just give me that deed and it'll be okay. Everything will be back where we were before you showed up at that hearing.

Oh Shit, said Kirk to himself, just after leaving his friends place. *I left my computer at Zoe's.* He looked at his watch. 7:30.

"Hey," Zoe answered on her cell. "Hey," Kirk echoed. "Guess what?"

"I'm looking at it. Next to the door. I'll bet you are home already?" "Almost."

"Tell you what, I'll meet you at the Caladonia Pizza place on Waialae tomorrow at 7 before we head back to your place. But I need to stop at my apartment for that."

"Thanks, you are awesome. See you then."

***

Crack. The partly rotted door to Kirk's apartment did not take much to open as a shadowy figure entered.

****

Chapter 18

A SHOCK IN THE DARK

Monday, February 27, 2012

It was only 10:00 pm. Still early for Zoe, but it had been a tiring day running from one end of town to another. Then up to Manoa and back down to Chinatown. Seeing the Mayor of Honolulu and then the "Mayor"of Chinatown.This happens when you have five assignments and three stories due the by six that day.

Zoe always nabbed her story. The three were done, and she left for her daily workout at Ala Moana Park. She ended it with a dip in the warm waters. No turtle today. Well, she lucked out only once a week swimming with the old guy that still comes out and keeps the lap swimmers company. Of course a lap was a half a mile for the length of the small bay, and Zoe knew she shouldn't have done it twice. Sure, she would feel good and for a while she would be refreshed, but she would pay for it later that evening and beginning to nod off and finally falling asleep, not to awake until morning.

But it was okay today. She felt a lot of stress and this was so relaxing. And she woudn't be meeting Kirk until 7. He said he had some things to research and would have to talk to some "old dudes" who must have known Captain Cook he said. Recently, he'd been crashing at her place if he was too tired to bike home.

Kirk was always a gentleman about it. He would always sleep on the couch if she was already in bed fast asleep. And though she wanted to wait up for him, she had already nodded off before the 10 o' clock news started. So she crawled into bed and was fast asleep.

She could just remember thinking about how she and Kirk had met, and how he asked her if she knew of a place he could stay for a week because of some special research, and how he didn't want the museum staff to know what he was doing. She didn't ask. When it came to intimate personal details, she was not the investigative reporter, but someone who gave her friends the space for their own lives and secrets. She trusted Kirk and asked no questions. He was such a contrast from other men she'd known. Nothing like the creepy Museum director, with suggestive sexual hints.

Instead she said, "You can stay with me." "I can't do that," he said.

She let a girlish giggle saying, "It's not like you haven't been at my apartment before, you know."

He put his head down a little answering, "Okay, but just for a few days." And in looking up, showed a big smile.

That was the last thing she saw in her mind's eye when she dozed off and was sound asleep.

The phone rang and startled her. The bedroom phone had a loud ring because Zoe was always afraid that she slept so soundly she wouldn't hear the ring. And she kept a landline in case she forget or misplaced her cell phone. She never wanted to miss even the slightest chance of getting a story. She didn't get many calls, but the few she got in a month were worth it.

This ring somehow seemed especially loud. She jolted up and wondered what was happening before the third ring. Then she said to herself, *Oh! The phone.* As she got out of the bed to go to the small desk to answer, she said to herself, *I guess Kirk isn't back yet, but he's probably sleeping in the living room on the couch* – she reasoned as she answered it. The luminous clock said 1 am.

The voice at the other end said in a very official way: "Are you Zoe Lee?"

"Yes, who's calling and why so late---errr so early? Calling from overseas?"

"This is Sergeant Clark at the Police station. Do you know a Kirk Daniels?"

"Yes, he's a friend of mine."

"His card lists his family in Sacramento and you, Zoe Lee, in Honolulu, as people to call in case of an emergency."

"Are you there, Miss Lee? We need to have you come to the station please. I know I've inconvenienced you, but it's important." His voice had changed and was no longer so official.

"I'll be right down."

The Hawai'i Commercial Daily
Wednesday, February 29, 2012

Museum Researcher Dies in Bike Accident

Kirkland Aaron Daniels, a junior researcher at the Cook Museum, died of injuries when his bicycle left a slippery road near his home in Palolo Valley. He was 28 years old. Daniels, a native of Michigan, is survived by his parents, James and Sharon Daniels, of California. Police reported the death as an accident. According to Honolulu Police Detective Sargent Stanley Takahashi, no foul play is suspected. Cook Museum Director Dayton Apo issued a brief statement: "Our Museum Ohana is greatly saddened by the untimely and tragic loss of Kirk Daniels. He was a gifted and committed scholar of Hawai'ian history. He will be missed. Our hearts and prayers go out to his family and friends." Funeral arrangements are pending.

Chapter 19

SOMETHING SMELLS ROTTEN IN PAHOA

Thursday, March 1, 2012

"Mr. Chang, could I see you when you have a few minutes to spare me?" Clare Song asked, as she poked her head into Charlie Chang's office.

"Ah my dear Ms. Song, I will be at your forensic lab pronto. But first I am to finish this memo to the chief," he said with a smile. "Be there in 15 minutes."

"Our poor boss, he has priority even before you! Another luncheon tomorrow! You may have noticed, he's put a few more pounds this year. I remember when he could slide through the bars of a prison cell."

"Come on, he was never that skinny!"

"I never want to be chief. In fact, he not only has to go to the luncheon, but this time he has to give the luncheon address. So he asked me to write some pointers on how we do investigations. But he said make it exciting. It's so boring these investigations, not like on television".

"Not for you Mr. Chang."

"Ah my dear Ms. Clare. Something is up! You never address me formally unless you have sniffed out something that everyone else has missed. Something is rotten in Pahoa, huh? Big Island, Kilauea."

"Everywhere you smell it. Smelly air. Can't escape it. And it's not just the volcano's sulphuric acid smoke I bet."

"I'll see you soon, Mr. Chang."

In 15 minutes Chang was in the lab. "So what have you found?"

"Well, I always look over the investigation reports that come in.And when it comes to Takahashi, I look at all of them even if they are classified as accidents. Mainly he's so sloppy, and you know me: everything has to be tidy. I try to help every officer, but he has never met my standards."

"And recently, you did ask me to be especially careful with anything he turns in that comes across my desk. Well, he was sent out to that bike accident where the rider died. You know the one several days ago?"

Chang was really interested now. He said, "The one that happened in Palolo Valley? The one where that Daniels kid was found dead?"

"Yes, it was a cold and wet night. The lighting is poor in that area to begin with, and one of the street lights was out. It was estimated that the so-called accident might have happened after 10 pm. Traffic is very light at that time. It's a working class neighborhood, and also filled with seniors who stay home."

"It happened near the small bridge over the stream. Takahashi believed that the bike skidded and caught the edge of the asphalt road, and slid into the border filled with rocks. He lost control, and then hit the muddy part of the edge, and since the water has an incline to follow into the stream, he went over the bank into the stream filled with a lot of big rocks. It's not a deep stream - maybe six to eight inches. So, apparently he crashed and smashed his head. He died instantly from head wounds. He wasn't wearing a helmet."

"The police report said the cause of death is clear. The investigating office, Officer Takahashi, concluded it was an accident - the rider was careless. It was late; it was raining; he probably wanted to get home and wasn't careful."

"Takahashi was out there with another officer, a rookie cop. They brought in the smashed up bike. It's in the pound. The next of kin can, of course, claim it."

"Well, I decided to take a look at it. Now, I found scratch marks on the rear fender. You couldn't quite make it out at first but it seems like the fender had been dented. Now this was a used bike. It wasn't a racing bike, and I think it was a bike you use to carry things since it had side baskets."

Chang said, "An archaeologist maybe who liked to collect things and inspect them at the office, or at home."

"Precisely," she said imitating Chang. Clare made a funny look and then said, "You know, I hang around you and Moto too much. Sometimes I sound like him too."

"So it's an old bike" she continued, "and it had a lot of small dents and a lot more scratches. But Chang, most of the scratches are all rusted over. These are new. Very recent. No rust. Like something hit it, a car actually. And one more thing. It was clear that Daniels died from a head wound. But I looked at the preliminary medical examiner's report. Daniels also had a massive black and blue mark on his back. As if, and I'm speculating here, he was actually struck by a vehicle."

**

It was about two hours later that the old yellow Datsun station wagon pulled up near the bridge. Chang did not tell Clare, but he had gone there on the same day that Takahashi had made his investigation. The bike was already gone from the scene.

He had several emergencies, and the Chief had been after him for some other investigations, including a major robbery and two manslaughters. It's usually peaceful in paradise, but when things happen, they seem to come all at once. So when he finally made it to the pound several days later, the bike was gone. The custodian said a family friend signed out for it. Chang checked, and it was just an illegible scribble.

He thought to himself: *Fortune smiles on us Moto-san. Clare got to it that afternoon and she took pictures in addition to her first hand inspection.*

Chang didn't want to go out to the site without bringing Moto. Moto had a different set of eyes. Saw what others missed. And lately, they found they enjoyed working together. And he didn't want anyone to spot his well-recognized DeLorean. He waited until after the lunch crowd was gone and clean-up had begun. Moto picked him up, so he too could see firsthand.

Moto looked at everything. He walked down the road. He looked at the streetlights – kind of dim, but still not completely out. He walked the bridge. He bent down to look at the condition of the road, the sides, the off-road gravel and rocks.

Then he spotted something that caught his eye. There were distinct tire marks on the side of the road, as if a vehicle had swerved onto the soft shoulder. Crumpled up in one of the ruts was a white piece of paper. It was a napkin with writing on it. He picked it up. The writing was a phone number. What was more astounding was where it was from: his very own Toronaga's! He showed it to Chang, who carefully placed it into a small plastic sandwich bag for preservation. Chang used his new smart phone to take a close up picture of the tire tracks. He noticed they were on the same side of the road where Daniels was found.

Finally Moto spoke. "In Palolo, city too lazy to clean roads. It's not rich road in Kahala. Tire marks. Trash. They stay around. Napkin could be new, could be old. You know, before we visit scene, Moto think those scratches on bike - it could be accident. No background on the victim, you would say like Takahashi it was just accident."

"But napkin and tires tell maybe different story. And not as dark as some said. Still get some dim street light. Maybe Kirk is victim. He make some powerful people angry. Takahashi chief investigator. You are quite right Chang-san, something rotten in where? Pahoa."

They were riding back together to Toronaga's. Neither was talkative. Then Moto spoke: "Wasn't rotten place somewhere in Europe?"

"Not Rotterdam. Moto, is that why you've been quiet all this time? I thought you were trying to figure this thing out like I have."

"Chang-san, Moto needs more facts. Plenty more facts before make educated guess."

"Well Mr. Moto-san. First you never make guesses. You know the answer even before you say anything. But for me, I always tell you look for the motive. The facts will fit in. Anyhow it's been sometime since we matched up notes and thoughts and suspicions. You know I think I'll be quite hungry later tonight."

"Ah, you want your usual late night second dinner? Or will it be third dinner?"

"Real funny, Moto. What time should I come? I know Shilling goes to Toronaga's all the time. I don't want him to see us together."

"Shilling comes maybe 5-6 times a week. Never stays later than eight. So come after say 9:00, depending how hungry you are. The last diner is usually gone by 10:30."

"I guess Shilling and the misses like to eat dinner early."

"Oh Shilling-san never bring wife to Toronaga's. I have never seen her."

"So he only brings his business buddies and the rich guys he's trying squeeze out of their money for his projects."

"Most of the time, but he come with women too. Only one at a time."

"So you going to call that number on the napkin?"

"No, I think I'll have an IT guy at the department identify it first. Don't want the owner to know that we know…not yet. More important might be any DNA ID."

Chapter 20

HE SENT MAIL!

Wednesday, March 14, 2015

With the death of her best friend and lover, Zoe Lee was determined to dig deeper into the circumstances of his death. It took some time to haul herself out of bed in the days after the shock, and just to eat. The long telephone call to Kirk's parents, filled with mutual sobs, had been a kind of release, and somewhat therapeutic. To distract her from her grief, she set her sights on being a reporter again, but this time it was very personal.

She was convinced, in some vague way, it had a lot to do with Kaka'ako, and the rights to develop it – not to mention the box with the Mahele deed that Kirk had come across. Wanting to know everything about what happened, it was frustrating that through some twisted sense of fear, he wanted to protect her from "certain knowledge" as he put it. He had showed her the deed once, but was determined to hide its identity from even her. *Too many spy movies,* she thought to herself. They had told Sheri and Kekoa, and at least Sheri had agreed with their stupid scheme. But now Kirk was gone, and she had no idea where he hid the deed.

The newly created "Urban Park" in Kaka'ako, just across from the Hunter Office Emporium, was no more than a narrow warehouse space with tables and internet connections. Zoe often went there to think, and to write. Coffee from the next-door bread shop helped. The man who invited her was already sitting at the back table – and with him a salt and peppered, almost hippie like older Japanese, sipping a takeout green tea.

"Inspector Chang? I'm sorry for being late…traffic."

"I understand. Please sit. Condolences about your friend Kirk Daniels. This is Mister Fujimoto, who often helps me out. He runs a local restaurant. Just call him Moto."

Zoe nodded to Moto tentatively. Moto smiled and nodded back. "Thank you for your thoughtfulness," said Zoe, "but how did you know about us? And why did you ask to meet? I've already spoken to some officers."

"I am taking over the case. I already have a lot of background information about the two of you from staff and friends. And just to let you know, I am part of your loyal following. I greatly admired your investigative work on the lack of security in plant shipments to Hawai'i. The poor inspection has allowed a lot of unwanted and dangerous insects to come here. Our poor honey bees and our endangered wildlife and trees. Auwe!"

"I know you are one smart hard-driving wahine. Some people might not like some smart reporter investigating and writing about their business."

"Could you not be so obscure? Please say what you mean."

"Have you noticed anyone or anything unusual? Any people or cars that keep showing up. You know what I would call intriguing patterns?"

"Well, come to think of it, there is this old beat up yellow Nissan."

"Never mind the yellow car. That's my friend Moto's car, keeping tabs. It was not a Nissan back in the time he bought it, it was called Datsun. So Moto still refers to it as his Datsun. We all humor him."

Moto nodded.

"OK, well, I keep seeing this weightlifter type of guy, really well built, kind of like a football lineman. I've seen him several times, and only noticed it really this morning when he actually bumped into me leaving my apartment. Do you think it means something?"

"He is not a friend. He could be dangerous. I see you have a laptop computer with you. Always carry it around with you?"

"Never leaves my side, why?"

"Moto thinks this man may want the computer information. Might enter your apartment. Might try to steal the computer. Might even hurt anyone there to get it."

"Well, I do have a good lock on the door, you know, dead bolt and all."

Moto spoke for the first time. "No problem for this man. If wants enter, he enters. He experienced." There was something about this soft spoken man that made Zoe feel at ease. Something about his gentle eyes that invited trust.

"Are you saying he is a threat?"

"Could be a threat", answered Chang. "Do you have good friend can with couch to sleep on for a while?"

"Are you suggesting I avoid my apartment?"

"Precisely. Moto think, and I think, you should not go home for a while. Maybe try not to be yourself. Buy some new clothes, visit a sick auntie or other friend. Don't take chances. We don't know what this man could do."

"Why should I become a fugitive in my own town? And for how long?"

"Moto and I are not sure, but at least one week, maybe two. Oh, and don't drive your car or your moped."

"You knew I had a moped?"

"Moto Datsun gets around," Moto added with a shy smile.

"Does this creepy guy have a name?" she asked.

"Name Kono. Here my phone number," offered Moto. "If you see Kono again, call right away. Moto give you a safe place to stay."

"OK. Well, I guess, thank you, Moto. You know this all sounds so crazy to me. Are you sure you are not overreacting? I mean, do I really have to move out, like right now."

Chang responded with authority in his voice. "You need a backup computer. You need to check previous emails from Kirk. You need to move. You need to disappear. Moto will drop you off to anyplace you need to go."

Chang pointed out to the street, where, previously unnoticed, sat a yellow Datsun station wagon.

***

Since Chang had mentioned the computer, Zoe remembered he'd left it at her place. She decided it was time to look at what Kirk had sent out and received in the last few weeks. If she had to, she would go back till when they started dating, a good six months ago. Who knows? If the info was there, she could go back to when he still lived on the mainland. Kirk was a very nice guy, but he took hard positions on issues. He was always ready to take a stand, and he didn't care what it might have cost him.

Zoe sighed. I think that's one of the reasons I liked the guy from the beginning. You always knew what was on his mind, and where he was going. Yeah, what did they say back then: No shibai from this guy!

She had the computer on, and noticed there was hardly anything on it. Either he hardly used it, or it had been erased. But he had to use it, because she constantly got emails with thoughts that had just occurred to him. He was always so involved that the messages were always quite lengthy.

I wonder what was going on? What was he thinking? Maybe he hid the hard drive and had a substitute put in. Or what else would he have done?

She kept thinking. I went through all of his papers. He liked to doodle and write notes, but I couldn't find anything except those where he scribbled my name. She sighed again over this memory of Kirk.

Oh I know: he stored important word documents and emails on thumb drives. I remember him carrying one once. Where would those be? I got a few of his boxes. She went looking for them and she guessed right. There was a small box of thumb drives.

Ever since Kirk had received the English translation of the document from Prof. Miller, Kirk became almost paranoid, she remembered. He told her that after making copies of the papers in the box, he had stashed them away where no one could find them. "Once Shilling knows what we know, he might try to find them and destroy them," he had reasoned.

"Well where did you put them?" she asked.

"No, Zoe, maybe I've been watching too many spy movies, but if they know that we are together, they may target you or your computer as well. Its better that you don't know. But don't worry, I'll leave you a clever clue in case you need to find them."

That conversation had really pissed her off. But in retrospect, she thought maybe Kirk had a fear that there was real danger. She wondered if he sensed something he would not, or could not, share.

She'd spent hours going through the flash drives. Nothing. Then she remembered something he had told her about his life in California. Kirk and his surfing buddies had created a kind of private club, where they shared their own secrets, and especially gossip about girls and surfing. On a lark, they all got their own separate emails with pseudo names. "Whenever we wanted to plan a party without our parents knowing, we'd use these emails. They never could figure it out," he'd explained.

I wonder, she thought. She started going through the hundreds of emails she'd received in the last few months. As a reporter, she got all kinds of tips from people she didn't know. Often it took her a long time to sort through them and delete the dead ends. She went to her account and started scrolling for something, what, she didn't exactly know.

Wait. What's this? Abigaleprinter@lava.net was the sender. Who the hell... She opened it. It was a short poem:

My daddy wore black, and his fingers were too
My Mother came as helper, but soon died of the flu.
He spread his pule far and wide, the first to find out how
The good deeds we know and see, near dear Kawaiahao.

What the...could this be one of Kirk's convoluted clues? Sounds like the kind of stupid and clumsy rhyme he might write. OK, so what does it really say? The only direct link to anything was Kawaiahao, as in the church, not the church per se, but near the church. Daddy in black, maybe a missionary. But who? Wait, the cemetery, the old one behind the mission houses. She shoved her laptop into her pack and set out on her moped with purpose and anticipation... not knowing exactly what she was looking for.

***

Zoe's adventure to Kawaiahao Church did not produce any flashes of insight. She was drawn to the crumpled ancient wall where the city bus had struck and dislodged the koa wood box. It was still surrounded in yellow tape from the police. It takes months to get anything fixed in this town. After an hour or so, she returned to her walk-up apartment. It was made mostly of cinderblocks, which literally held and radiated the day's heat well into the night.

When she arrived, she parked the moped and walked up to her third floor apartment. She stopped in her tracks, the front door was ajar. Cautiously, she peeked in. She cleared her throat and coughed, letting any intruder know she was there...just in case. Not a peep. She snapped on the light and looked in. The apartment was a total mess. Papers, clothes, everything strewn about. Dresser drawers were pulled out. In the kitchenette the cupboards had also been opened. Pots and pans were on the floor. Even the refrigerator had been opened.

Whoever did this wanted me to know...wanted to send a message, she thought as she dialed Moto's phone number. He did say he lived nearby, and would always be available if she needed help. He answered and told her he'd be there in five minutes.

Chang arrived only minutes after Moto. After inspecting the scene, Charlie Chang agreed with Moto that this was not only someone looking for something, it was also a message...a warning. Zoe, as strong and confident as she was, had seemed visibly shaken. "Someone is trying to hurt me," she kept repeating over and over. It was without hesitation that Moto convinced her to move into a back room at Toronaga's. "No one will ever suspect you are there, and you will be protected," he said.

"Moto think something more you want to tell us, yes?" They were in the back room of his restaurant.

"We had no idea it would come to this," said Zoe, searching the eyes and expressions of Detective Charlie Chang and his friend. "We were going to give the deed to the Kalani family in plenty of time to claim the inheritance."

Chang stared expressionless at the young reporter. Not a muscle moved. He sat erect in his chair, his usual habit when he wanted to convey serious disapproval and formality. He said nothing, letting Zoe squirm. Moto was looking thoughtfully at the ceiling fan lazily turning in his restaurant's private office. His gaze drifted down to the scroll with Chinese characters on the wall – a quote from Lao Tzu's Book of Tao – *He Who Speaks Does Not Know He Who Knows Does Not Speak.*

Finally, Chang raised his head to look directly into Zoe's eyes. "You thought you were smart. You thought you could play with people's lives. You thought good intentions were enough. You were cavalier with the law. You are precisely accountable for the consequences. What is your excuse for your stupidity?"

"Please, that's, that's just not fair. We had no idea..."

"Moto want explanation too. Tell full story now."

"Look, this stuff just happened. We, Kirk, was told by Apo to investigate this koa box found in the wall – you know – when the bus hit it, I think it was ah, December...

"Just the facts. Don't try to soften the sordid tale with irrelevant details," snapped Chang with ice in his voice.

"Kirk opened the box. He found documents. We took them to the UH prof who knew what they were, and translated the Mahele deed for us. I knew that just finding an old deed probably would not have any impact on an actual development. Titles and ownership would have been settled long ago. A lost document like this may have historical value, but…"

"But smart twenty-somethings have scheme to give deed artificial power, yes?" asked Moto.

"Yes. We thought there must be a way to use this. We could think of nothing. But then the notice in the paper after the death of the movie house guy – the land goes to the Museum OR would go to anyone with a valid Mahele title from the 19th century. The light bulb went on."

"So you saw an opportunity to shake up Shilling. You knew that if you could find the real owner of the deed, a pretty iffy possibility, you could stop the development. It probably would not happen. So you took out insurance – gave Shilling a way out – just pay to get the deed – when he would then destroy," intoned Chang, focusing on the logic and the motivation.

"That's pretty much it. Kirk went to Shilling, actually met right here in your place Moto, and made him believe we were for real, had a deed, and it had a price. All along we planned to expose him for bribery, or at least really discredit him. But then…"

"So now you are an expert on criminal bribery? And when, young lady, did you intend to tell the Kalani family about all this?" *asked* Chang.

"Actually, we already have. Met with Sheri and Kekoa who sometimes works at the coffee shop. Turns out the land under the shop is the land owned by the projectionist, actually his uncle. His girlfriend Sheri knows. We know each other from high school soccer days. But we can't prove anything without the original deed. The lawyer says our translated English version is of no value. The will is the will."

"Kirk like Zoe too much, Moto think. Protect girl, keep in dark, hide box and deed, make sure, just in case. Then someone took care of the problem, took care of Kirk."

"And," Chang began, "now we have multiple problems, thanks to a stupid reporter and her boyfriend. We have a possible murder of Kirk. We have a ticking time bomb in desperate attempts to find and maybe destroy the deed before the six months run out. We have one reporter, one Detective, and who knows who else, trying to find the deed. And we have likely a poor Hawai'ian family that might not get their land."

"And," added Moto, "Museum have motive to destroy deed. Shilling have motive to destroy deed. All kinds people have motive to destroy deed. All kinds people motive for finding deed. All angry, emotional, self-interested people on both sides."

"Precisely," said Chang.

"I know. I know. I can't tell you how bad I feel, all this, on top of losing Kirk. Is there anything, ANYTHING, I can do to help make some of this right? Anything?"

"Moto think, Chang-san, maybe one thing, keep girl busy, maybe find something."

"Personally I think she has messed up enough," snapped an unsympathetic Chang.

"Just hear Moto out. Where box is, we don't know. Let girl help find. If can, can. If no can, no can. Moto see no harm."

"Yes, please Detective Chang. Let me dig around in the background. Maybe I can find clues or directions from emails or papers left by Kirk. One thing I know in my heart, he would have left some way for me to find it on my own."

"One problem," said Chang with just enough of a subtle softening to his harsh voice. "Zoe, you are now the main target of those who want to destroy the deed. Like it or not, THEY, whoever they are, will assume you know. Not only your home, your property, your very life may be at risk. You must continue to stay here in the spare room. You need to get new clothes, perhaps a disguise of sorts to make it difficult to spot and follow you. You need to have Moto here keep tabs."

"Yes, OK. I understand. But why don't you just arrest this Shilling guy and his thug friend?"

"We have no evidence against them. We have more than one suspect based on motive... We cannot assume anyone is innocent, or anyone is guilty. We need to know more, find more facts, and, as they say, connect the dots."

"Moto can play part. Must insist on cooperation. Zoe carry smart phone with GPS. Keep on at all times. Zoe call Moto twice a day. Zoe and Moto have code word to indicate danger...maybe phrase... can use without suspicion if someone in room listening...last words to sign off...if OK say Bye, if danger say...ta ta."

"Sounds all James Bond to me," said Zoe.

"Listen to Moto", said Chang. "Follow his instructions. If, at any time I feel you are not cooperating, you will be put on a plane to Chicago, where a good friend of mine will meet you at the airport and escort you into custody. Understand?"

"Okay. Okay."

"Now leave Moto and me alone. Please leave this room."

After Zoe left, Moto looked up from his yellow pad where he had been doodling notes in kanji.

"Well Moto, what is your best guess to sort out this mess?" asked "Chang. Shilling have motive. Gamblers like bus driver have different motive. Corrupt Detective Taka have motive. Even Mai Tai's have motive. Museum Apo set to gain if deed not found in time. Museum maybe want to sell land and nice price to friend Shilling. So Apo and Shilling have same self-interest."

"Precisely... Mai Tais who want to be bought out. Detective Takahashi who seems very eager to declare Daniels' death an accident. And he is pals with Shilling and Apo. More loose ends. More dots with no connection."

Moto picked up the office phone and ordered a specific brand and year of sake, along with Chang's favorite okonomiyaki pancake, Oaska style.

Chapter 21

··

SOMEONE IS ALWAYS WATCHING

Tuesday, March 27, 2012

Julie had her back to the row of drinkers at the bar. She casually washed and dried glasses at the sink, but her real purpose was to keep an eye on the clientele through the large mirror. "Had it shipped all the way from a saloon in Arizona," she bragged to anyone who would listen. Her bar was not in the best of locations for professionals, on the edge of the old Chinatown red light district off Hotel Street. But looks can be deceiving. Behind the sawdust and the smell of beer engrained in the wood, Julie made it known that if you asked, you could order the finest Scotch whiskey, and high quality imported Shochu, and cabernet at $150 a bottle. "We are upscale seedy," she liked to say.

As a result, professionals who wanted to be discrete for a wide range of reasons' would sometimes appear at the door. They could get a booth if they were lucky, or a stool at the bar. This night, there were two men who seemed to need the discretion.

"Dr. Apo, my boss is getting worried," confided Kono, whose large frame barely could balance on the stool.

"Kono, I told Bob there is no change in our plans. Everything we agreed on will be ok."

"Boss says too many people know too much. He has a lot of money invested in this project. And there are too many snooping around, like the cop Chang, and that reporter chick."

"Look, don't get antsy. Don't do anything stupid. Everyone needs to keep their cool. Don't' make trouble when it isn't necessary, ok? Kono, tell me you haven't done something. No, No, never mind, I don't want to know. Keep me out of it."

The early evening was muggy, and the only breeze was from the musty ceiling fans and the open door. Apo looked at his watch, and emptied his class of scotch. "I don't want to be involved in anything that can upset the deal, any more than your boss." He put cash on the bar, and left ahead of Kono. Kono did not follow. He ordered his favorite shochu, and lingered for another fifteen minutes.

As soon as he was out the door, Julie carefully picked up their two glasses with a napkin and placed them in plastic bags. In each bag she placed a small piece of paper with the name of the customer. She stared off into a corner booth, and nodded. Charlie gracefully rose and glided to the bar.

"Julie, you are a pro."

"Charlie wen you gonna divorce that job and marry Julie, huh? We make good money, good money, and Julie treat you right at nite, you know."

"Julie, I've got to get out of here before you tempt me into something I'll regret," he smiled, taking the plastic bags. She blew him a kiss and he turned to bow at the door.

***

Two days later Clare Song called. "Charlie, we compared both bags. The one you labeled A was negative, but bag B was actually a match for the napkin. Hope that helps."

"I owe you a dinner at your favorite restaurant."

"Bali? Can't wait. And they have the best sommelier to pick out the best wine. They call him Stevarino. Let me know when you make the reservations."

"Precisely, good wine and good reward for the best forensic…"
"Forget the flattery Detective, just deliver on the meal."

Chapter 22

SECRETS OF THE DEAD

March 31, 2012

She was not an unattractive young woman, and her usual dress spoke of young, sassy, and pretty well proportioned, for someone on the thin side. It was not difficult to find loose jeans, a hoody sweatshirt, and a knitted ski cap to transform her into a young man with ear buds listening to music on his smart phone. She practiced walking the way blue-collar workers swaggered or lumbered. It felt strange and phony, but at least she wouldn't be taken for a young woman. Dark sunglasses completed the outfit. She waited until it was dark, after 8.

She had rented a different moped, and was zipping in and out of traffic on Queen Street past the car repair shops. First stop, was a small walk up where Shari lived. It took her time to scope out the cars that seemed to belong to the residents. There it is, in the stall labeled Resident Manager! Zoe turned off the moped, and looked around to make sure she was not followed, especially by Moto in his beat up Datsun. Nothing. She took out a small flashlight and began inspecting a Ford truck owned by Joe Davis. *Why does an overweight do nothing urban guy need a truck?* she asked herself. It was black and rusty in parts. Her eye caught the irregular front bumper. It was clearly dented and the paint scraped off. This was recent. No rust on the bare metal, she thought. She took out her smart phone and silently took several pictures of the front of the truck, including the license plate.

Her next stop was the usual hangout for the Cat Lady, but she was nowhere in sight. She headed off towards Kawaiahao Church. *Maybe I'll see something that will ring a bell,* she hoped without conviction. The churchyard was in shadows as the day was coming to a close. No tourists were strolling the grounds. She made a special point of looking at the now famous toppled lava wall, where the box that started this all was found. It was surrounded by yellow tape. Nothing new here.

She wandered around the back, to the ancient cemetery, where many of the original missionary families were buried. The stones were thin, many leaning to one side or the other. Then she remembered Kirk's obscure poem. She had it somewhere. Digging into her wallet, she found the small piece of paper.

> **My daddy wore black, and his fingers were too**
> **My Mother came as helper, but soon died of the flu**
> **He spread his pule far and wide, the first to find out how.**
> **The good deeds we know and see, near dear Kawaiahao.**

So what does this mean? What is Kirk trying to say? Oh Kirk you smartass, I wish you were here...

After searching the gravestones and reading all the inscription, Zoe sadly was ready to give up. She knew she was right, and the answer was here, but she couldn't figure it out yet. She decided to take a break and return on the next Sunday. It seemed a more promising time to search again. But then something struck her as interesting.

The good deeds we know and see, near dear Kawaiahao....

I wonder... Methodically, she started reading the headstones. Names from Hawai'ian history were everywhere. Then she saw it... "In Loving Memory of My Dear Abagail, Born, March 3, 1801, taken to Heaven by the consumption epidemic, February 10, 1831. There was no family name, but next to it another grave and both were surrounded in a low cement square. She read them out loud:

Reverend Malcolm Goodeed. Born August 15, 1795 – Died September 12, 1846. Good deeds we know and see…Goodeed, that's it! Maybe this is the clue! Who was this guy? She pulled out her smart phone and googled the name. Member, second group of Boston missionaries. Responsible for importing the first printing press. Printed the first King James Bible in Hawai'ian. Built the second of the existing mission houses behind Kawaiahao Church. Lived and preached on all Islands until his death of a sudden illness in 1846.

So what does this mean? What is Kirk trying to say? He's linking our box to this missionary, who was a printer and….wait…I think Chang or Moto might be able to figure this out….Oh Kirk, you smartass, I really wish you were here…

Chapter 23

GRAVELY SPEAKING

April 1, 2012

Charlie looked intently into Takahashi's eyes. "So Stan, you think all this rezoning was the work of Thomas, who after all was Shilling's godson?"

"Are you kidding?" Stan unwrapped his paper chopsticks. "If anyone knew what was going on, and why, and how, it was Thomas. Thomas was probably on the phone, trying to play the big shot who could deliver. Everybody knows he controlled the Commission. Some say they got certain benefits, but that's just hearsay."

"So maybe Thomas was more motivated and agitated about Kirk?" probed Chang.

"Are you kidding? Why, Shilling was telling me, ah, I mean, someone said they heard Shilling yelling at Thomas."

"Precisely! Stan, I appreciate your analysis. You have a good mind. Mahalo for sharing."

"Yeah, no problem, anytime. Oh, I see it's after 8, I've got another meeting Charlie, so got to go." He abruptly stood up awkwardly and began to pull out his wallet.

"Forget it Stan. This one's on me. Thanks for meeting and sharing." "Oh Stan, one more thing. You think there is any connection with gambling in all this, do you?"

Takahashi, in spite of being red faced from drinking, turned white.

"Never mind," said Chang, waving him out the door.

"Moto see Charlie look smug and satisfied. Perhaps Detective Stan tell something important?"

"Precisely. Takahashi confirmed that Leighton Thomas was becoming a problem…too talkative. Too over confident, especially for Shilling. Thomas claims to be his godson, but Shilling never really agreed. Still a useful tool. Oh, and one more thing. Stan was not happy to hear me mention gambling."

"Moto think Stan full of poppy poop. More important. Did you get results from lab?"

"More than that, I think Stan is trying to throw Leighton Thomas under the bus, make him a suspect in Kirk's death. Seems awfully anxious to shift interest away from Shilling."

Charlie removed an envelope from his suit jacket, which he insisted on wearing as if it were a uniform. He handed it to Moto, who read it and raised his eyebrows. "Not what Moto expected of DNA. What about the phone number on the napkin?"

"More dots to connect. Moto run into our reporter Zoe late at night sneaking back into our back room, all dressed in disguise. Cat Lady called earlier, says Zoe was spending time near the church. So Moto confront smart reporter. She not apologize, she all excited. She thinks the box and the deed are somehow connected to the Kawaiahao cemetery. She had her laptop and showed me Kirk's funny-kine email:

My daddy wore black, and his fingers were too
My Mother came as helper, but soon died of the flu
He spread his pule far and wide, the first to find out how
The good deeds we know and see, near dear
Kawaiahao.

"She thinks this might be an important clue. You think she's right, don't you?"

"Yes, Moto think she is probably right. We look there we might find box and original deed and Mr. Shilling's big project go kaput."

"Clare Song did a few favors for me other than the napkin and the glass, and the door to Zoe's apartment. Nothing inside. Someone we know put his mitts on an outside door. Big hands, big prints."

"I think you and I should go visit graveyard. Maybe we figure out what Kirk meant," suggested Moto. In a few minutes they were at the Kawaiahao Church Cemetery, at the Makai end of the church grounds. "A very historic corner, Moto- san. This is the corner of Queen Street named for Hawai'i's great Queen Liliuokalani, who was a member of the church, and directed the chorus, and who also wrote those great songs we all love, like The Queen's Prayer and Aloha Oe. She also wrote operatic pieces, I was told."

"And then it intersects with Punchbowl Street which goes towards Punchbowl Crater and Cemetery---The Cemetery of the Pacific. I always feel a part of history when I come here."

They decided to split up the coverage. Chang started at the mauka end and Moto started his search from the Queen Street side. They took their time checking the site and reading each gravestone carefully. It was agreed that if someone found anything remotely suspicious, or somehow related to Kirk's email, he would give a yell. The other would then rush over and the two would compare observations. After 45 minutes they met in the middle of the cemetery. No one had given a yell, not even the slightest peep.

"Well Moto-san. Looks like there's nothing here after all. Should double check each other's work and I do your side and you mine?"

"No Charlie-san. You and I think alike. I trust you were precise as usual and there is nothing."

"Same for me. I guess that's it. I'll go back to office and you will have to begin dinner prep."

"You know, Charlie-san. Everybody think this all to Kawaiaho Cemetary. But there is small grave area on the top side. Small graveyard near King Street and Chaplain Lane, the small lane connecting King and Queen Streets."

"Chaplain Lane. Hey Moto, now that's something. It must be there." The two men rushed over to the King Street side. Chang saw it. "I've never been here. Of course, I don't go to this church, just an occasional funeral service."

"You know, Charlie-san. Most people like you born and raised here in Hawai'i, or any other place, think they have seen all there is to see in place of their birth. But sometimes you miss a lot. Takes one malahini who come here to get into it. When I come Hawai'i, I read everything, I go everywhere, I make sure I know everything. Have to make up for all the years I missed by not being born here and raised as a kodomo."

They crossed the sidewalk and went into the graveyard. It was small. "Now Charlie before we start, you come see something with me. Whenever I come here I always check this statue." He took Charlie to end of the small graveyard and there was bronze of a woman bent over and holding her arm out. In her hand was a flower. She was mourning a deeply felt loss. The sculpture reflected the image of all women who were friends, or wives, or mothers, who lost someone they loved deeply.

Charlie was taken by the sculpture. He said, "Wow! How did I miss this in all my years?"

"When I see woman now, I think of Zoe. So young and full of hope and so much promise. I think, Chang-san, Zoe lose the love of her life. She will be like this woman. She will be great reporter, I know, but she will always remember Kirk. Maybe this more than symbol. Good omen. Look over there."

Chang peeked over one of the taller stones, and then he saw her. Zoe was standing writing down inscriptions on a gravestone. She saw them, and waved them over. She showed them the grave of Abigail, and then the phony email Kirk had used.

"Moto thank you for showing me this. Now we closer to solve this case!"

They started going through the graveyard together, checking out each gravestone. It was small and took so little time. No other grave marker clicked the way Abigail's did. "Chang-san, Kirk real smart boy. I know answer and what he did. Come."

Chapter 24

EVERYONE A SUSPECT, OR MOTIVE IS EVERYTHING

Tuesday, May 1, 2012

There was an eerie darkness in the Mission House, even with the lights on. It was just a little past closing time, tourists and staff had left, but remaining were those summoned by Detective Charlie Chang. They were sitting restlessly: Shilling and Kono, the Mai Tais, Dr. Apo, Kekoa and Sheri, Officer Takahashi, Leighton Thomas, and even the bus driver Henry Doyle. Except for the Mai Tais, no one was speaking, but no one could sit still either. And even the Mai Tais were almost whispering, at least for them it was a whisper, and only sporadically. Moto, who had asked some of the group to come, sat in silence away from the rest, near a dim window.

Shilling finally broke the near silence and said what was on everyone's mind. "So why are we here? Look Moto we have things to do; lives to live. Kono and I will be leaving in another five minutes."

"Chotto," said Moto, putting his hands up with palms facing the crowd. "Please, a little patience. Need just a little more time. I make this promise: You not be disappointed."

Just then everyone could hear Chang's supercharged De Lorean. Moto was thinking: there's that sound. The century old door swung open and Chang walked in, dressed in his usual black collarless long sleeved shirt, his image of a smart, neat, slightly formal, and no nonsense persona. Zoe was just a step or two behind.

Chang stepped in front of his audience and just smiled, not saying a word for a few seconds, which to some seemed like minutes.

Moto spoke. "Everyone here. Famous Chinese Philosopher once say all important events happen in short moments. But the time before seem like forever."

Chang spoke for the first time. "Mahalo. Everyone came on time. You are here out of curiosity, or maybe obligation, or self-interest, or perhaps, for one, fear. Now, why are we here? This is more than about an old deed. More than about profits. We are here to examine the facts surrounding the murder of Kirk Daniels."

"Murder? Murder?" the crowd mumbled in unison. "It was a traffic accident! The Police said so."

There was only one member of the crowd who had not joined in the uniform cry. That was Officer Takahashi. His face slightly reddened instead. He lowered his head slightly.

"Takahashi!" A low and raspy voice whispered with resentment. It was Shilling. "You assured me it was an accident. Or maybe a hit and run. And you're the officer in charge!"

"Yeah, the paper said at worse a driver leaving the scene of an accident," shouted the Mai Tais together.

"All what you folks have said is true. I am, or was, in charge of the investigation, but it looks like Mr. Chang here as superior officer went to the Chief," grumbled Takahashi.

"The Chief was persuaded that evidence and logic could lead maybe, just maybe, to another explanation," said Chang.

"Moto wonder why this young haole boy with so much to live for, especially with one smart and good-looking local girlfriend, is now dead. Why would someone or some people wish him dead?

What secrets did he hold that someone would want him to take them to his ancestors?"

"Our Chief of Police said that he is willing to trust where the evidence leads, namely, that someone or some people (gazing at the Mai Tais) went to a lot of scheming to eliminate this irritant. Or to put it in local vernacular, take plenty trouble to get rid."

As Chang began his oh-so-logical peeling of the onion, Moto watched the faces and the body language of each participant. He knew that when Shilling was nervous, he tried to affect an artificial swagger – sitting with his legs apart. *Swagger present in developer*, he thought. He knew when Joe Mai Tai was lying, he fidgeted his left foot. *Plenty fidget today*. Henry the bus driver tended to look only at the floor when he was uncomfortable. *Floor of much interest to Henry today*, he thought.Chang continued, "Mr. and Mrs. Mai Tai, your simple apartment building is an important piece in developer's lucrative condominium dream, correct?"

"Well I wouldn't say that," blurted out Joe a little too loudly. "His agents have made inquiries. Me and the Mrs. haven't decided...."

"Excuse me please," injected Chang. "You do recall the talk we had in the Chinatown market? The only question was the price. Only a foolish man would think that a multi-million dollar deal will be stopped because a small landowner rejected an offer of a few hundred thousand bucks? We are talking jackpot here. This could mean the difference between a comfortable retirement or an unpleasant move to a smaller rental apartment well outside of the city. This not like old Chinese laundry: no tickee, no laundry! This is more like let's make a deal."

"So you know you're going get your price to make the missus very happy", Chang continued. "She will become a Queen. All hail Mrs. Mai Tai!" Chang made a slight bow towards the lady.

"But then you discovered that perhaps you won't get to make a deal. Kirk Daniels, so young, thinking he's smart and in command. He couldn't stop talking to others about his move. And you were informed by Shilling and Kono of the threat to your pot of gold."

"Now you and the Missus worry. Maybe you won't make 3-4 million dollars," Chang continued. "In fact it could be much worse. You might end up not owning anything. You came to paradise, but paradise costs money."

"Okay, so I got worried, but I'm no killer," said Joe.

But fidget foot tell story that you maybe something else, thought Moto. Charlie added, "Motive is everything. If you have a motive, perhaps you find a way."

Joe could not resist defending himself. "So he had an old piece of paper. Shilling can challenge it. That's what I understand. But Detective Charlie. I know you checked things out. You know me and the Missus couldn't have done it. We were taking friends from the mainland to the North Shore, and we had dinner at the North Shore Bay Inn. You must have checked it out."

Joe's eyes widened. Molly's hand reached for his knee, squeezing it to restrain him from saying something foolish.

Joe glanced at Molly and took a deep breath. "And I spoke to Mr. Shilling. He said to keep cool."

Charlie turned abruptly towards Shilling, who visibly seemed to flinch: "Yes Mr. Shilling. I will get to him. But not yet."

Moto again was thinking to himself. *You sly one Chang-san. You always planned to start with the Mai Tais. It wasn't the sequence of events that was important. No, the Mai Tais are the appetizers. You just want people hungry for more. A grand feast!*

"Precisely, supportive and loyal friends. Maybe you went back to Honolulu and came back on that fateful night. Not much traffic at night. But let's move on."

Chang turned in a semi-circle, now confronting Takahashi.

Moto interrupted. "Officer Takahashi. You bad boy. You wrote in your report it was accident. Either you're one sloppy policeman, or you're trying to protect someone."

Takahashi, ignoring Moto, looked directly at Charlie. "Come on Chang. Why would I do that? What's the motive? I have no land in Kakaʻako. I don't gamble. I don't have debts or owe any favors. I didn't have any reason to want to stop Kirk, or promote Shilling's development. The Mai Tais have, and of course Mr. Shilling has the biggest motive of all," shot back Takahashi."

Moto interjected "Happy and honored see you patronizing Moto's humble restaurant, Toronaga's. And happy you joined by friend Mr. Shilling – more than once. Maybe you want something else from him. Maybe time to retire with nest egg. And now you say motive---Mr. Shilling, your friend, has the biggest motive. Moto think throw friend under bus."

Chang took over again. "But what alleged motive? Maybe you found out something. Could it be that Mr. Shilling's alibi for the night of the murder did not check out? Is there a little scent of blackmail here, for self-interest of course."

Moto saw Takahashi all of sudden lost the defiance in his face, become subdued and looked to the floor of the Mission House as if looking guilty.

"So let us come to you Mr. Shilling."

"Look Chang. I don't know why anyone is pointing their finger at me. I could have cared less about Kirk Daniels or what he claimed he had, said Shilling defiantly."

A chorus of voices blurted out: "You lie. You would have lost hundreds of millions. You would have been ruined. Bankrupt!"

"Please let's be civilized." Injected Chang. "We are examining motive and opportunity. And so what is the motive? What is Mr. Shilling's motive? The multimillion dollar development that Kirk Daniels was threatening to stop by coming up with a threat to ownership of the land? That's big, right Mr. Shilling? But you were not worried even though the Mai Tais and everyone else might think so. Now why is that?"

Shilling was unwilling to lose control of the story: "Because when you do a land deal of the magnitude of this one, you properly check out all the details. The sale of the land was first listed in the Mahele Book in the 1840's and officially recorded. Back then you recorded land sales and purchases in what is known as the land court. The documents are often hard to find because this was long before computers and everything was on paper, easily damaged, easily lost. And many of the land deeds and sales were recorded in the original language of the parties--Hawai'ian and Chinese and even Japanese in a few cases. So my lawyers checked it all out. But long after that, clear title was determined, and the owner was this Peter guy. Any older deed is worthless."

Joe and Molly Mai Tai said in unison: "Then why did you bother to even listen to Daniels?"

"Well, obviously, the posting of that last will, that said the land either goes to the Cook Museum or to anyone with a valid original Mahele deed. He said he had a deed. Normally, it would have no weight, but this will could have changed everything. Of course, I didn't believe him. What is the likelihood that such an old deed would show up from a Hawai'ian family? But I thought I would play along, and let him think he had the goods on my development. And, if it came to a lawsuit by environmentalists and Hawai'ian advocates, I could make them look stupid, and even hopefully get them off my backs for future projects. Hell, I would demand they pay my legal costs."

"Moto moved by poor, innocent Mr. Shilling", he said in false sympathy. So, Mr. Shilling had no motive for killing Kirk. His development was safe. "So why did Officer Takahashi see him? There's something there."

"Smart boy. Mr. Shilling," said Chang. "So you're not worried they going to stop the development. In fact, maybe you wanted them to try. So, if you have no motive for the murder of Kirk Daniels, why were you worried? Why was your henchman Kono stalking people?"

Shilling had his head down, rubbing his hands together. He looked nervous and was silent.

Chang continued. "You worry because you could not be sure Kirk was BS-ing you. Could it be your alibi didn't check out? You say you were home, but you were not. When Takahashi checked with your wife, she was shocked because you told her you working late at the office. Perhaps if she found out about late night drinking, checking out the ladies at hostess bars. And in fact when she found out, she threw you out."

"Leave my wife out of it. Yes, I was worried about the initial bad publicity. It's one thing to have the environmentalists try to stop you, the investors are used to that, and they know my history. But to be accused of, what? Something unsavory? Something criminal? That's serious, bad politics, and maybe fatal to my project. Even if I eventually cleared it up, the investors might have reason to pull out. This was the biggest deal of my life."

Moto smiled to himself, as Chang had used an emotional and personal issue on Shilling to trigger a statement of more serious motivation.

Shilling wasn't done. "So Officer Takahashi came to see me after checking with my wife, and he said I was now in trouble. I told him the truth, that I had no reason to fear Kirk. Yes, I should not have toyed with the young man and led him on. Takahashi said maybe he could help. I told him, I remember favors. I don't forget my friends. He didn't tell me how, but later I read about it, and Kono here did do a check, and Officer Takahashi did conclude the death was an accident in his official report," said Shilling with an air of confidence.

Chang stroked his chin thoughtfully. "Speaking of Mr. Kono…"

Recognizing immediately his vulnerability, Kono said, "Hey, I'm just a driver, just a flunky here. I just provide special services to my boss, Mr. Shilling here."

"Moto know about special services. Like stalking Zoe. Like breaking into apartment to send warning. Moto wonder about other services…"

Kono whispered something to Shilling, who shook his head.

"I can assure you, Detective, I would never authorize any criminal activity. If Kono did something on his own, well."

Kono flashed his eyes at his boss, what local would call, stink eye, as if to say 'Hey boss, don't throw mu under the bus. I'm loyal. You remember that.

Chapter 25

THE MISSION HOUSE TREASURE

Chang continued. "As part of our investigation, we sent our crime scene team to every place that might be connected to the murder" of Kirk Daniels. We sent our best. I never work with anyone but the best - Clare Song. We know that Kirk rode a bike on the night in question. We know he died that night. And now we know that some people were in the neighborhood. Anyone in the neighborhood would have had the opportunity to hit him with a car." "So when Clare and her team went to Kirk's apartment what do you think they found? Fingerprints. Yes, finger prints on the door. On the doorknob. Clean fingerprints, and lots on the panel of the door to his apartment. Surprise! Whose prints do you think we found?"

Chang swiveled suddenly and leaned forward. "Henry Doyle! You were there. Admit it."

"No! Mister Chang! Yes.. but... yes I was there. But no, I did not go in."

Chang wagged his finger. "Come Henry. You had an interest in this whole business with Kirk. If not for your stupid no- paying- attention to driving, the bus would never have hit the Kawaiahao Church wall. There would be no deed. We would not be here. Kirk would still be alive."

"Yes," answered Henry, speaking very subdued now. "Yes, you're right. I wish I could have a chance to do it all over again. Who would have thought it would all lead to this? And Zoe, I am sorry. But…"

"Come on Henry. Cut out the fake sorrow," continued Chang. "Oh Zoe, I'm so sorry. You had a different interest in the deed, but not like the others. You wanted to make sure the deed was not lost or destroyed. You heard that Kirk was maybe going to give the deed to Shilling for a price. You didn't want the property sold at all. You believed that if Kekoa got the deed that he would keep the land. There would be no more sale. No more billion dollar development. And most important to you, your favorite gambling places in the area would continue to operate – the ones who still gave you credit. No worry Henry. I know your credit history, about the credit here and loss of credit everywhere else. Moto-san here, he has his ways. He checked you out, and he got it all from the operators. Where you go before you got suspended---Chinatown, Kalihi and that place by the airport." Henry sank his head with each place name.

"Okay Mr. Chang. I won't deny all that, but I didn't go inside and I didn't do any harm to Kirk. I wanted to go in and check out the place. First, I waited. I figgered Kirk was bound to show up after maybe an hour. Yeah, I wanted to break in. I came close. I was even shaking the door to get a feel for it. Then I stopped. I had enough trouble for now. My luck was still bad. So I left."

Chang paused for a few seconds. "Ah! But others were there. Others were in Pahoa, with their cars." He stopped, and let the silence build up. He didn't look at anyone in particular. He gazed up at the ceiling. Charlie left it to Moto to look at the audience, who focused only on three individuals. He wanted to see their expressions. He was not disappointed.

Chang, as if on cue from the director, slowly spoke. "I said there were fingerprints. On the door panel itself. And not just Henry's. Others!"

"Okay! Mr. Chang! A voice shot out!

Ah, good Kekoa. You honest boy after all!

Kekoa confessed, "I was there, too. Only, I didn't know about Henry or anyone else. I must have come after he left. Everybody knows my interest. So there's no need to hide. Yes, I went. I wanted to talk to Kirk. I was going to plead with him to give me the deed right away. Okay, sure I got angry at times. I thought here's another haole just taking advantage of us Hawai'ians. Yes, I was determined not to let that happen."

"But I wanted it man-to-man. I knocked. Doorbell wasn't working. I knocked maybe six, seven times. Each time louder. I tried the door knob. I must have left my fingerprints. I have nothing to hide. I did try to listen for sounds, talking, music, and television coming from the apartment. So yes, I pressed my body and ear against the door. I heard nothing. So, I assumed he was still out but thought he would be returning. I even checked under the door and I could see what looked like a few letters and mail in the slight crack between door and floor. These are old apartments you know. So I knew he hadn't come back."

Kekoa, you one smart boy! Thought Moto to himself.

Kekoa continued. "That's all I did Mr. Chang - I just waited. I must have waited maybe 45 minutes, not more than an hour I'm sure. I left. Sorry Sheri, I should have told you. I just wanted to protect our…" Sheri gave him one of those looks, meaning *we are going to have a conversation about this.*

"Someone did go in and left a mess, papers strewn, furniture upended," said Chang. "How can I be sure it wasn't you?"

"No, Mr. Chang! I wouldn't go that far. Yes, I wanted that deed. It's mine after all. Yes, I got angry. Yeah, really mad. I admit that, but still---I would respect his space just as I wanted him to respect my property. I decided I would go up to the Museum after classes were over the next day and confront him there. According to the public notice, I still had time. I was mad, but I was still a long way off from going nuts, and I was not desperate."

"But not so for someone else in this room. Am I not right Mr. Thomas?"

Thomas let out a sudden and soulful moan. "Oh my God!!" Even Chang and Moto expressed shock in their faces. Everyone else had a look of some fear at the unexpected emotional outburst.

"Yes it was me!" Holding the sides of his face in distress, Thomas continued. "I did not kill him, but I am not without sin. He died! My actions must have contributed! Oh good Lord! I am so sorry! Have mercy on this humble sinner. Did I, in my heart, wish him harm?" He broke out into uncontrollable sobbing. It took a while before he stopped. No one knew what to do. Chang looked puzzled.

Finally, composing himself, Thomas spoke. "How did you know Mr. Chang? I did go up to the apartment. Yes, I was there. But I just parked in the guest parking stall. I was just waiting for Kirk. I expected him in just a few minutes, since I had passed him in the dark. But I just stayed in my car. I was talking just to myself, and to God. I wanted him dead. No, I *wished* him dead. I wanted God to strike him down for what he did to me. And for stopping me from going on to do His Work. I had big plans Mr. Chang. I wanted to do God's work. Kirk put an end to it. Mr. Shilling promised me land to open a church. I was going to do good. I was going to change my life. I dreamed about it every night. So, when the dream was dying, maybe I thought Kirk deserved what he was getting."

His eyes rolled as he looked at the low ceiling of the small sitting area. He began rambling as much to himself as to the others. "No! NO! I just said words, I didn't mean that. But then he didn't come home, and I knew he was coming to his apartment that night. So, I knew my wish had been granted. I knew something bad had happened. I was so scared. I didn't mean it. I was just angry. I didn't mean it. Oh Zoe, I'm so sorry. I really didn't mean I wished he was dead. I didn't really want God to strike him dead. But I knew it had come true because as I drove back, I don't know how long I was there, but I saw the police cars. There had been an accident. I knew that would have been the way Kirk would take to go back to his place. I did it. I contributed. And I didn't mean it. But Mr. Chang, I did not go up to the apartment. I just stayed in my car."

"Chang looked at Thomas pathetically. "True. I believe you. Ms. Song did not find your fingerprints on the doorknob or against the door like Doyle's and Kekoa's. But you were talking to yourself out loud. The manager couldn't hear what you were saying, but he did see the other two 'guests' and he figured you were also coming to visit Kirk. So he wrote down your license plate number, just to be safe. That's how we know. "

Chang swiveled to direct his gaze at another in the room. "But Honorable Chang not finished yet," he said for the benefit of the Mai Tais.

Moto rolled his eyes. *Oh no. Chang-san trying out his Charlie Chan imitation again. Keep telling: you not so good. Forget.*

Undeterred by his friend's gesture, Chang continued. "I think this person maybe had a different, more personal motive than the rest of you. More than one motive, means more than one possible suspect. Sometimes the obvious is not the truth. Isn't that right, Dr. Apo?"

Apo, who had been feeling relieved and was visibly shocked when Chang had suddenly turned his attention to him. "What are you talking about? I have no interest in the development. I don't even know Mr. Shilling, except on the occasion he made a sizeable donation to the Museum and when we had the annual Mahalo Party, he showed up along with hundreds of other donors."

"Ah but Dr. Dayton Apo, you had not one, but two motives to want Kirk Daniels to, shall we say, go away?"

"What are you talking about you crazy Pake?" Chang did not react to the slur.

"Motive number one, initially, perhaps a handsome additional endowment from Shilling and friends to pay for new research projects, and to help you build an international reputation. But even better, with title to the land, you could sell the deed to anyone, perhaps even, Mr. Shilling. So maybe the Museum gets the land, then sells it to Shilling. Everybody is happy and rich."

Chang added, "You knew Kirk's fiancée, Zoe. When you guest taught at the University, maybe once a year, you met a vibrant and attractive young wahine, and became infatuated with Zoe when she was doing her graduate work. You have a great reputation with young wahine students. During the semester, you even took her to dinner. After the semester was over, I learned you gave her the highest score possible. You again asked her out. I am sure my friend Moto was honored you chose his Izakaya for your hopeful date. Over dinner, you talked about your feelings for her. She stopped you, and told you that she did not want that kind of relationship. She thought of you as her respected professor, and that was it. What a blow to your ego! I was told no co-ed could resist you."

Moto looked at Zoe. She nodded. "That's right. He came on to me. He hated Kirk right from the start because it was obvious I was more interested in him."

Chang picked up the story line. "She thought, and very naively in the beginning, that your interest was professional. She said she believed you liked her research ideas. She said she was, how they say, involved, with Kirk, and unavailable. She wrote this in an email to Mr. Daniels that night. Documentation. Facts. Finally, realizing her mistake at agreeing to dinner, she said she came that last time just to tell you personally. Then she left. You're just by yourself… at the table…just feeling stupid… I wonder what you were thinking."

"Months earlier Kirk came to work at the Museum. Maybe you thought, Eh, just another haole boy who talks too much. Maybe useful, maybe not. But as time went on, Kirk began to tell his co-workers that he just met the girl of his dreams. Overhearing this conversation from time to time, you knew he was talking about Zoe. Then several months later, he even said her name. Kirk was probably the kind of young man who was so in love that he talked big about the lady he would marry her someday. You're a very competitive person, from your past record. You always had to be tops in your class in the classroom and on the field. But we won't go into that."

Chang paused to let his narrative set in. "It was when that box was brought to you, that you hatched a mean plot that would involve Kirk. You saw the deed. You read about the public notice and the will of the Uncle. Oh, you already knew there might be deeds like that, especially for parcels in Kakaʻako. You knew there had been a lot of Hawaiʻian claims in the 1800s. You had even been hired to supervise archeological digs in Kakaʻako. And you, being a thorough person, probably checked the chains of titles of the parcels. You would have done so, because of your proud Hawaiʻian heritage. "No more will haoles going to come in and steal again," you've said that at Native Hawai'ian conferences. And here was a haole boy stealing one of "our women" again. So I'm thinking…."

Apo blurted out, "Stop all of these lies Chang. You don't know what you're talking about. I thought you wanted me here to help your case against one of the others here. You made no mention that I'm a suspect. I'm leaving. You have no proof. No proof at all."

"Dr. Apo, I know you were at Kirk's apartment. Was it you who broke in and tore up the place? For a trained archaeologist, you should be ashamed of yourself." Apo was beginning to fume now. Attacking his academic credentials was not something he expected, and after the charges about a failed romance with Zoe. This he was not expecting. This he thought was private.

"Surely, Dr. Apo, if you treat artifacts and ruins like you did Kirk's apartment, you would have been kicked out of the profession. Why, they would take back your doctorate? You do have a doctorate, don't you? I guess it must be so since we have to call you Dr. Apo. Hah! Doctor……." Chang was pushing the motional buttons.

Now, Apo was visibly angry. His face was what one might call beet red. "You god damn Chinaman."

"No, Dr. Apo, I know you were at the apartment, not because there were fingerprints inside. I did say there weren't any, but look here. We found a cocktail napkin with Toronaga's name and logo. See? He held it up. Right Moto-san"

Moto responded "Hai!"

"How sloppy of you to use this cocktail napkin right after you saw Mr. Schilling. Look, your handwriting. You wrote down Kono's cell number. I verified it earlier. Yes, you absent mindedly took it out and wiped your fingerprints, but that's not where we found it.

Apo shot back. "That's a lie. He angrily stood up. "I didn't leave that napkin. Why would I wipe out my fingerprints? I wore gloves when I went there. I always wear my archealogi…" His voice went silent as he realized what he had just admitted."

"Ah, so the Honorable doctor was there. You have admitted that in front of all of us. Now, Dr. Apo, I am not asking you to say anything. You listen like everybody else."

"Bullshit! I'm leaving." He turned.

Before Apo realized it, Moto, a six-degree black belt in Aikido, moved effortlessly towards him, blocking his path to the door. Apo turned quickly, and he raised and drew back his arm. He swung his right fist forward aiming at Moto's face. Moto deftly blocked it, and with minimum movement, grabbed his hand and twisted it in such a way that brought Apo to his knees in pain, and spun Apo around gently but firmly twisting both arms.

"Now, do not give me cause to allow Sensei Fujimoto to make it more painful", said Chang. Chang went on as if it just a momentary distraction.

"Now that we are more reasonable. You gave temporary custody of the box and its contents to Kirk. Later, when you realized there was a tentative connection to land development, you thought, maybe you'd let Kirk reach too far, discredit himself. You knew from his prior statements at the first hearing that he was opposed to the Shilling development. He was one of the leaders in the environmental movement here, and that he might jump to the wrong conclusions, and think he could use the deed to stop that billion dollar development. The truth would sooner or later come out, and not only would he and maybe the environmentalists look stupid, but this would also deny him admission into any of the better doctoral programs. None of the elite graduate programs would want an idiot like Kirk on their campus. And he would not get any grants or teaching assistantships if there was a damaging letter from a former employer. A failure, you were sure Zoe would dump him. You were so confident of his arrogance and ignorance, you didn't even bother to tell Shilling. Not until you saw the notice of the will did you know your scheme had backfired."

Chang did not pause long enough for another response from anyone. "And as we all know, there is a connection between this box and two of our young guests tonight – Kekoa and Sheri."

The young couple, just nodded. Sheri now held Kekoa's hand as if to give him support. Kekoa straightened his back, raised his head, and was determined to learn all he could about the fate of the box.

"I, of course, read the will. I knew Uncle Peter was really into history and Hawai'i issues. I knew he wanted to donate his land to the Museum. When I saw the part about the deed, I figured it was just something he threw in, not really expecting it to happen."

Chang continued the story. "It was only later when Zoe told you that they had discovered this box with an actual deed, and it was to your coffee shop property."

"Moto think, first tear up office and apartment looking for box. Look like was just robbery. You could not find. This made you angrier. The next day at work comes what great philosopher calls the straw which breaks back of a camel."

Zoe spoke. "Kirk told me, and everyone who would listen, that both his office and apartment were trashed. He wondered if it was because of his opposition to development. Kirk said he thought that Shilling had sent Kono out to "get him." When co-workers warned him about going back to the apartment to live, I told him it was OK to crash on my couch. Frankly we were getting kind of serious. Kirk was, well, ready to move to the next level in our relationship. I guess he started to tell others was that he might be staying at my place for a while until things calm down. Said it saves rent. Kirk was thinking about it."

"Thank you Zoe, for that," said Chang, who turned back to Apo. "That night, you went to the Pahoa apartment. You looked for, but could not find the deed. On the way back down the valley, perhaps you spotted Kirk on his bike. It was a dark night. It was raining. How convenient for you. You saw him. You could easily make it look like an accident. So you did it."

Chang continued. "No one focused on you, or even thought of you. You had no direct known interest in the development. Your car was never checked by police."

"You have no proof," snapped Apo.

"Ah yes, proof. How foolish of Director Apo to lose a napkin on the road near the murder scene. The napkin, it turns out, has your DNA on it, and Kono's private cell number on it. You were there, you had motive. And, to add to the evidence, your car fender had a fresh dent with paint scrapped off. But not all the paint. A tiny bit of paint that matched exactly the paint on Daniels' bike."

"Like I said in the beginning. It all comes down to motive and opportunity. In the end, only you had the both the necessary motive to want to commit the crime of murder, the opportunity, and the carelessness to leave evidence of your presence at the scene. Dayton Apo, you are under arrest for the murder of Kirk Daniels!"

When Chang said that, Apo leaped out of his chair, and he was out to strangle Chang this time. Chang stepped aside while throwing a punch to the midsection to knock the wind out of him. Apo went down gasping. Two uniformed officers that had been waiting outside the historical wooden mission house now entered, handcuffed Apo, and led him out the door.

"Ladies and Gentlemen, I'm so sorry for the violent display. This was not supposed to happen."

The Mai Tai's could not restrain themselves any more: "Wait, Charlie, what about the box? What about the deed? Does it really exist? Where is it?"

"Please accept my humble apology. We meet here at the Mission House because Kirk was a smart boy. He knew someone was out to get the box and the deed. He hid the deed, but left obscure clues with Zoe. Zoe, will you do the honors?"

Zoe, stood up facing the semicircle, the former suspects. "Before that, I have something to say to all of you. I still cannot grasp that I have lost a person I might have spent my life with. He was strong, he was committed, he was…sweet and kind. All of you somehow represent people who, in my view, lost their way, lost their compass in life. The Mai Tai's – so fortunate to live in paradise, yet so unable to see their own good fortune. Mr. Shilling, so devoted to making money, so indifferent to who could get hurt. Sending your henchman, Kono, to do some of your dirty work. Detective Takahashi – a lifetime of public service now tarnished for what? Gaining favors with a developer? For me, you have taught me some valuable lessons, some of life's pitfalls to avoid. But I am more determined than ever to carry the spirit of my Kirk into the future, to be an honest and fair reporter of the truth, and to hold people accountable for their acts."

The room was silent. Molly was dabbing tears off her cheek. Sheri was nearly sobbing.

Zoe continued: "He hid the box here at Mission House, in the old printing shed. Now it sits before you in plain sight." She pointed to a simple wooden table off to the side of the room. On its second lower shelf was a decorative, polished koa wood box. They all looked. A quiet gasp.

Zoe picked up the box, opened the lid, and removed a very old and slightly stained paper. She handed it to Chang.

"I hold in my hand the deed to an important parcel of land in

Kaka'ako," announced Chang. "It is a parcel that includes the land under Uncle Peter's coffee shop. Its owner is a Hawai'ian family that received this royal deed nearly 150 years ago. It was originally hidden, as we now know, inside the older coral wall of the church, exposed by Henry Doyle's bus accident. How ironic that Uncle Peter's will resulted in a deed that will keep the land in the hands of his own relative, Kekoa."

"I would like to now happily turn it over to the new, legitimate owner, someone whose right to this land has been confirmed by lawyers who examined the will. Kekoa, this is yours! Well, you can look at it for now, but we will have to hold it as evidence until all of the criminal proceedings are over. And believe me, there will likely be more than one criminal proceeding. Then it is yours and your family's forever.

Kekoa Potter stood, accepted the paper. He looked at it with disbelief. After what seemed like an eternity, Sheri leapt up and gave him a huge hug. They turned to Chang and Moto and got more hugs and smiles.

The others quietly left the scene of joy and filed out of the two-hundred-year old Mission House.

Postscript

....

THE MANOA INVESTIGATOR

Thursday, June 16, 2011
May 23, 2012

MUSEUM DIRECTOR CHARGED WITH MURDER

Developer Implicated in Cover Up.

By Randy Grossmann

In a scandal that rocked Honolulu's economic, political and cultural worlds, one of the most respected members of the elite, Dr. Dayton Apo, has been indicted for the murder of a member of his staff. According to court documents, Apo intentionally struck Kirk Daniels, 28, while the victim was riding his bicycle near his home. A police spokesperson declined to say what the motive was, but insisted that there was clear forensic evidence brought before the gran

In a story broken by *The Manoa Investigator*, it was revealed that the well-known developer Robert Shilling was also implicated in efforts to harass and intimidate landowners who could complicate or block his development plans. Chief Investigator Charlie C. Chang told reporters that Shilling may also face charges of obstruction of justice and bribery. He also said police were looking for a former Shilling employee who may have assisted in the cover-up.

The death of Daniels was apparently related to the discovery of an ancient, yet valid deed from the era of Kamehameha III, which, through the provisions of a landowner's will, would be honored in a way that prevents Shilling from moving forward with a major project. Following the indictment, the chief investigator for the police, Detective Stanley Takahashi, abruptly retired from the department, citing a desire to spend more time with his third wife. *The Manoa* has learned, however, that Takahashi was forced out because of a relationship with both Shilling and Apo, and because it is suspected he intentionally filed a false report that Daniel's death was an accident.

The Manoa discloses that its award-winning reporter, Zoe Lee, had a personal relationship with the deceased, and, according to police, contributed to solving this case. Ms. Lee is on administrative leave.

Epilogue

ALOHA MEANS FAREWELL...

Zoe you picked a wonderful spot for Kirk's grave." It was Kirk's mother, Sharon. She spoke with tears in her eyes, looking back at the recently covered gravesite. She could, at first, not comprehend that fact that her son had been found on the side of the road, apparently having crashed his bike on a slippery road and fallen into a ditch. But then to learn he was murdered! He was so young, and so full of promise. After meeting and getting to know Zoe, both parents agreed that burial in Hawai'i was what Kirk would have wanted.

His dad was holding on to his wife's hand with his head slightly bowed agreed. "We made the right decision. We and the kids all agreed that it would have been Kirk's choice too. He was here for only a short time but he loved Hawai'i. He said he was going to make Hawai'i his life-long residence."

"Zoe, he said that before he had even met you, Sharon added. He'd never leave for sure. Kirk sent out tons of emails. But for us, he always wrote. That was his sign that whatever he was telling you was of the greatest importance for him. Once you two met we got a letter a week."

"This place is so historic," Zoe said. "The Oahu Cemetery with many famous, but not of royal birth, people. The famous Alexander Cartwright who wrote the rules for baseball is buried there."

"I'm born and raised here, and it was Kirk who told me that. He took me there and showed me how people would make what he called pilgrimages there and leave baseballs and sometime even baseball gloves to honor the man. Cartwright started the first public library in Hawai'i too."

"And down the street is someone I'm sure Kirk would have liked to have met, Joseph Campbell. He's buried there, and wrote about heroes and quests. I think Kirk was always on some quest."

"Well we better go to the reception and meet all the people who came again."

The father added, "I'm amazed that so many of his schoolmates and all of his old surf gang flew in."

Charlie Chang and Moto were at the upper edge of the Pali Graveyard. They were too far away from the gravesite to hear them speaking. "They need their privacy," Chang said.

"Moto so glad we ease just little the pain Zoe carries."

"Yes, tough girl. She'll carry on. She'll always hold Kirk in her heart though.

"You know Charlie. Times like this, so happy we have Asian heritage, if you understand meaning."

"Moto-san. You are such a philosopher. Yes, who knows? Maybe in the next life, Zoe and Kirk will be together, and this time they will have a happy ending.

............Until We Meet Again.

Authors' Notes

All characters are fictional. References to the division of lands under the Great Mahele, and descriptions of Kawaiahao Church and the damaged wall are true and well documented historically. The incident of a bus striking the wall was a real incident in 2012.